My Mine or Yours?

A novel from the files of

Eric Bonfield

Private Detective-Geologist

Book 2

By

Max W. Reams

Books by Max W. Reams

Geology of Illinois State Parks

A guide to the physical side of 28 must-see wonders of Illinois

Oil on My Hands

A novel from the files of Eric Bonfield, private detective-geologist: Book 1

Before your Journey

A Premarital Study Guide

On the Journey

A Married Couple's Study Guide

ACKNOWLEDGMENTS

I am grateful to my thoughtful and insightful volunteer readers. I especially acknowledge the editing of Eric Bowles, Charles Wray, and Carol Reams for moving the story along. All errors are mine.

DEDICATION

This book is dedicated to Carol, my wife and chief encourager, and to our children, grandchildren, and great-grandchildren.

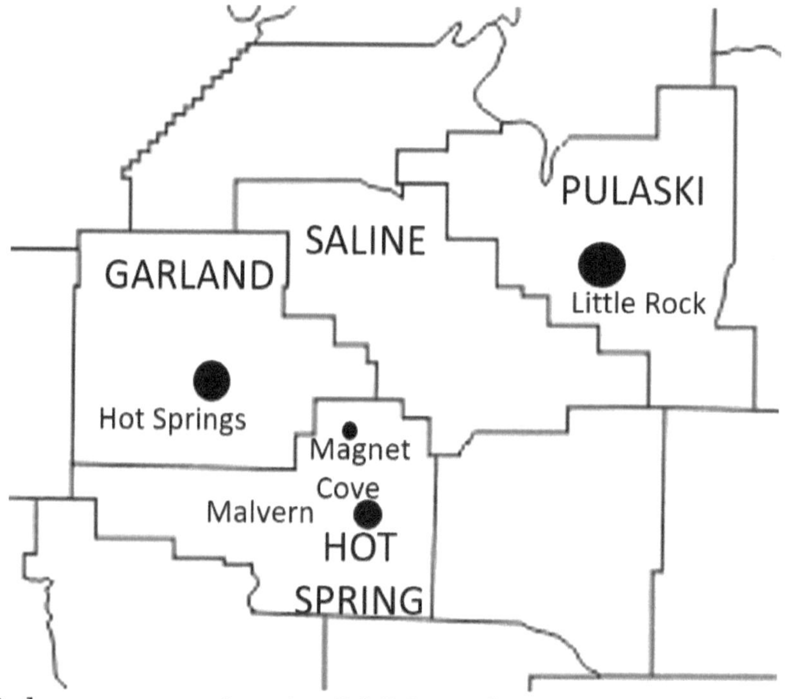

Arkansas counties, in CAPS, and towns/communities mentioned in the text. Modified from: © https://d-maps.com/carte.php?num_car=19684&lang=en

Chapter 1

Eric Bonfield stumbled to his pickup. Grabbing the pickup door handle he paused to shake his head, showering the parking lot with shards of broken glass. "What'd I do to earn this?" he muttered. Acrid smoke from the burning Jag filled his nostrils. He choked as he inhaled and tried to spit the nasty odor out of his mouth. *No luck.*

Why was the Jaguar blasted by a car bomb? Was my new client the target? Eric smiled grimly. His client had driven out of the restaurant parking lot in a beat-up Chevy pickup with a nondescript Arkansas license plate dangling from the rear plate holder. A few moments later, a beautiful black Jag parked by the café entrance blew apart in an incendiary explosion that shattered the restaurant's windows and sprayed glass over lunching customers and their food.

I thought the Jag's owner was my new mysterious client. Eric's first guess when he arrived at the café for the secretive lunch meeting was wrong. *Nope, my client drove a broken-down pickup with a good 20 years on my F-150. Why would one of the richest men in Little Rock putter around in that junk heap? Whoever planted the bomb must've made the same mistake I did in trying to identify the banker's car.*

Eric's lunch meeting was shrouded in secrecy. A phone call to meet with the prominent bank executive was all he had to go on. As he surveyed the still smoldering vehicle, Eric's mind tried to reflect on the previous couple of days . . .

****

It was Tuesday, and the air conditioner puffed to remove humidity from his pickup on that July morning in central Arkansas. June had successfully lulled the state's residents with comfortable temperatures, but they paid for it now as midsummer struck. The vehicle's radio warned of violent thunderstorms with obligatory hail and damaging winds. *Wish it was still June.*

He grumbled his thoughts on the way to a remote café far outside the sweltering city. When Megan, his office manager, handed him the phone yesterday, he listened to a strange request.

"This is Sean McDonnell," said an unfamiliar but authoritative voice. "I've an urgent need for your services. I'll call you tomorrow about a lunch meeting. Keep this under your hat."

Puzzled, Eric reluctantly agreed to meet the caller. *What's so hush-hush? I hate secretive calls wanting professional help. Such calls often smack of work at the edge of legality.* He avoided these like the plague.

Promptly at 10:30 a.m., Tuesday, the call came through. After a very brief conversation, Eric held the phone limply in his hand. He looked at his watch and knew the caller precisely judged how long it would take to reach the rendezvous location. *I've got to leave right now!* "Have to go . . . urgent," he said over his shoulder as he rushed out the door.

Megan sat at her computer wide-eyed. She turned to Joseph, Eric's business partner, and said, "When was the last time you saw Eric leave in that much of a hurry?"

"Not since Sarah was kidnapped!" Joseph said. "Do you know what's going on?"

"No. All I know is the caller's name: Sean McDonnell."

"Should I know him?"

Megan straightened in her chair as she prepared to deliver a lecture on members of the upper crust in Little Rock. "Sean McDonnell is a prominent businessman in our fair city." She proceeded to educate Joseph on Little Rock's big wigs as Eric drove rapidly out of the parking lot. His tires squealed on the already warm pavement. Joseph sighed and settled in his chair as he resigned himself to Megan's lengthy enlightenment speech.

As he paused at a traffic light, Eric mumbled internally. *What does Sean McDonnell want with a geologist who does private investigative work? Is there some business deal that needs consultation services, or does he have a missing family member? I'm not used to working with such high-level individual clients. Big corporations or small individuals . . . those are more my style. I hope it's on the level. I've had my fill of shady companies.* After the light changed, he gave up trying to guess the reason for the meeting and just drove.

If McDonnell had called a day later, I wouldn't have to miss lunch with my fiancé. Well, Sarah isn't exactly my fiancé yet. That'd be jumping the gun. He and Sarah were a serious couple, but they weren't much closer to engagement than they'd been months ago. Eric's emotions wished to be farther along in their relationship than his mind permitted.

His conflicted schedule began this morning. He arrived at the parking lot and pulled into his usual space at 7:45 a.m. Locking his pickup's door, he glanced around the lot. Sure enough, Megan's car occupied the choice spot nearest the door to his office. *Typical. She always beats me to work and takes the best parking place.*

Ever since Megan moved from part-time to full-time, Eric could never get to work before her Chevy SUV rested comfortably in the coveted space. *No use trying.* He sighed as he walked up the office building steps. Then he smiled. Eric knew Megan would be waiting to pounce on him with a boatload of work. She'd grin widely at his facial expression when he noticed the stack of projects displayed in the middle of his desk. *I can't keep up with all the stuff she gives me to do.* Megan enjoyed staying one step ahead of Eric. She liked to keep him busy. Entering the office, he grinned at the fun-filled employee and glanced at his workspace. Eric's eyes opened wider than usual at the huge pile facing him. Megan chuckled out loud and turned to her computer, secure in her morning success.

"Oh, by the way." Megan rotated her chair to face him. "Did you turn on your cell phone this morning? Sarah called here."

"Oops, I forgot. I always turn it off at night to avoid late scam calls waking me up. Guess I forgot to turn it on this morning." Eric sheepishly dialed her number. "Hi, Sarah, what's up?"

Sarah's smooth voice cooed, "Just wondering if your schedule is too full for a lunch date?"

"Of course not!" Eric answered quickly.

She suggested his favorite restaurant, and that sealed the deal. He hung up and turned to Megan, "I don't have any lunch meetings scheduled, do I?"

She shook her head, shrugged her shoulders, and said, "Nobody except the richest guy in our capital city!"

Eric's chin dropped.

Megan knew that Sean McDonnell would not be denied an audience with Arkansas' well-known consulting geologist with a knack for solving crimes. She looked at Eric over her glasses and smiled. The day wasn't starting out as he planned.

"Ouch! I'd better call Sarah back!" He quickly punched in her number and apologized.

Sarah allowed Eric to swim in guilt just long enough before she let him off the hook and laughed. "You'd better meet your new client. Who knows? Maybe this'll be the next Arkwell Oil case!"

"I hope not! That one about cost both of us our lives. I'd prefer a much milder assignment."

"Got to take what you can get," Sarah said with a mild chuckle. Her practicality mixed with humor showed through the phone.

After he hung up, Eric looked at Megan. "You know, I've got a problem turning my phone on in the mornings. Could you please remind me to do that?"

"I would, except you don't have a landline for me to call!"

"Guess I've got to remind myself." He resurveyed the mound of work on his desk. "I probably don't have enough time to start a new project this morning, so I'll work on an old one before that lunch meeting."

"Sounds reasonable," said Megan. She turned to face her computer screen.

****

Well, that's the way it started. I hope this meeting is worth the trip. After maneuvering through busy downtown traffic, Eric entered I-30 headed west. This part of the journey was fine, but soon his GPS exited him onto a state road. Suzie was the name Eric called the voice on his GPS. She quickly turned him onto a county road. This was followed by several turns onto roads that were successively more challenging. Potholes and washouts appeared without warning. *Guess folks in this part of the Highlands don't invest much in highway improvements. Wish I was headed to a fine lunch so I could gaze into the beautiful eyes of a pretty brunette.* A pothole encountered his left front tire, and the shock jerked Eric out of grumbling about missing lunch with Sarah. He frowned. *Bad road. Why meet a prominent businessman at such a remote outpost? There're plenty of nice places in Little Rock right next to his bank building.*

Sean McDonnell's reputation as a banker was well known. His bank held more assets than any other in Little Rock. Eric returned to thinking about this secret meeting. *What would a geologist who investigates crime be to this man? Was this guy expanding into mineral resources or oil or some other geological commodity? All he said was "to keep this under your hat". Not for public consumption.*

Then Eric stretched his shoulder muscles and gripped the steering wheel for leverage. The next pothole lurched his pickup to the right. *Got to have the front-end alignment checked . . . these backroads in Arkansas are brutal.*

He chided himself for being too cautious about new, unknown ventures. Eric's popularity as a private investigator allowed him to choose jobs that matched his expertise and interests. He took the same approach to geological consulting work. He avoided requests that stretched his personal morals or professional ethics. *There's enough honest work around to keep me busy. Money? Not a problem. Cracking the Arkwell Oil case solved that issue. Joseph and I can barely keep up.*

Finally, after miles of driving over roads that rattled his truck and Eric's bones, the mystery café appeared on the right. It was partially hidden by blackjack oaks. The setting appeared picturesque in a rustic sort of way. The exterior décor matched the wooded environment. *What's a nice place like this doing in the boondocks?* Eric pulled his pickup into the nearly full parking lot and noticed a black Jaguar amid humble Ford and Chevy pickups. He managed to find a spot far away from the café door. *Business must be good for such a remote place; probably the food. And that Jag's got to be my client's.* He walked up the steps and into the restaurant. *This building's anything but a dump.* The interior dining area was tastefully decorated. Wait staff wore well designed uniforms. *I'd expect this kind of stuff in downtown Little Rock, not in rural Highlands. Where's the money come from to do this?*

I don't know what Mr. McDonnell looks like, but said he'd be wearing a blue shirt. The only customer remotely matching this description wore a blue plaid shirt and jeans. He was balding and not very tall. Somehow the attire didn't match Eric's expectation of a prominent businessperson. He approached the man and introduced himself. Sean McDonnell displayed a professional banker's smile, offered a firm handshake, and encouraged Eric to have a seat. As soon as Eric sat, he immediately learned something about Mr. McDonnell. *This man wastes no time.* Business-mode ruled.

"I understand you're a geologist who does private detective work."

"That's a pretty good description."

The waiter came and took their orders. Since McDonnell ordered the daily lunch special, Eric followed suit. *Sean McDonnell doesn't flaunt his wealth at business lunches.* Eric knew a few truly wealthy people. One common characteristic often stood out; they worked hard for their money and didn't waste it. Many followed the principle that, to be wealthy, frugality hovered over everything. They put their money into high level priorities; they avoided trinkets and false appearances. McDonnell fit this category well, or at least his choice of food and clothes suggested it.

Getting to the point, McDonnell laid out his concern, "I've got a problem with some property near Magnet Cove."

The mention of Magnet Cove immediately piqued Eric's interest. This small area east of Hot Springs holds one of the most fascinating mineral localities in the eastern half of the United States. The Cove produces very unusual minerals and attracts companies taking advantage of economically valuable ones. As a graduate student at the University of Illinois, Eric emphasized petroleum and natural hazards in his studies, but mineralogy also fascinated him. During one of the geology departmental field trips, he roamed the haunts of Magnet Cove. He collected minerals found in only a few places on Earth. The geologic conditions necessary to form such natural materials made this a must-see stop for serious mineralogists.

McDonnell began an animated discourse, "You see, a number of years ago, my brother, Abe McDonnell, bought this piece of land. It's only 80 acres in the backwoods not too far from here and has little farm value. He and his wife lived on this property for many years. He was a handyman and sometime cattle breeder. Everybody in the area knew Abe and he was well-liked. His farm is mainly wooded with enough grassland to support his hobby of raising cattle. I remember he could fix just about anything mechanical. This is all just background.

"Change came when a person claiming to be a geologist knocked on Abe's door. He suggested there might be valuable minerals under the ground on Abe's land. This person said he represented Overshoot Mining. The company wanted to lease Abe's property. He must have tempted my brother with a percentage of the proceeds from such a venture. Apparently, they struck a deal. I have no details on any of this."

After shifting his weight and sipping some water, McDonnell continued. "I didn't pay much attention to what went on. We McDonnells are a large family, and our personal independence is highly valued in the tribe. I stayed out of my brother's business, and he stayed out of mine."

The banker looked pensive. "Abe's wife passed. He went through a tough time and I didn't hear much from him. Then one of the relatives told me Abe died and left me his land. That surprised me and everyone who knew him. I don't know why he did it. Others in the family aren't well off and could have benefited from the property. I don't need the land, but Abe apparently had his reasons. The problem is mineral rights. My brother didn't leave those rights to me."

Eric's brow furrowed as the waiter brought their rather scanty meals. "Mineral rights usually transfer to the heir along with the land. Who's got the rights?"

"It seems my brother left the mineral rights completely to this Overshoot Mining Company. Something smelled fishy to me. I'm not one to let what looks like a shady deal slide by. So, I'm in a legal battle with Overshoot Mining. From what my lawyers tell me, the outcome is uncertain."

Eric sympathized with McDonnell before he bit into a sandwich. "I don't know why you need my services. I'm not a lawyer."

Putting down his sandwich, Sean McDonnell stared directly into Eric's eyes. "Mr. Bonfield, I want to know two things. First, did my brother Abe know what he was doing when he signed the papers that gave away the mineral rights to someone outside the family? And second, what's this company doing with the property? I figure the first question falls in line with your private investigating skills. The second question is about geology. Am I correct?"

Eric blinked and thought for a minute before responding. "Mr. McDonnell, I highly doubt that an answer to the first question can be found. That would require locating people who could testify, with certainty, that something was wrong with the will or how it came about. To discover that might take a lot of work, and it's very possible the question may be unanswerable. The second one might not be so difficult. Documents filed with the state should tell the story."

His potential client leaned forward with a firmly set jaw and said, "I agree that my question about Abe's state of mind may be difficult to unravel, but there may be witnesses who can provide an answer." He paused, apparently gathering his thoughts.

"Now, about the company's use of the property. Overshoot Mining told the state that they're in an early stage of development, and it may be years before anything comes out of the ground that can be sold. Their reports seem very evasive and provide no clue what they intend to do or what they're doing right now, for that matter."

Eric mentally scratched his head. *This project comes in two very different flavors and requires two very different approaches.* "What about your brother Abe? You must know enough about him to make you question the will's validity. You say there may be witnesses. Are these relatives or friends who might know what condition Abe was in when he signed the documents?"

"I don't know anything for certain about what Abe was thinking or if he knew what he was doing when he signed on the line. We didn't talk much. But, yes, there're relatives who might know something about what went on at the time. Will you take this case so my lawyers can have something to use in court? I want to reverse this mineral rights thing. And I really want to discover the company's purpose in digging on the property."

Should I take the case? The prospect of snooping around Magnet Cove is intriguing. That amazing bit of land has puzzled geologists for years. The unusual minerals there are interesting. Curiosity and the love of a challenge tickled Eric's mind. He responded with a nod, "I'll try to find answers to your questions but can't promise anything. The mineral rights documentation will probably be the most difficult nut to crack. If your brother was not of sound mind, the will granting mineral rights to this company is invalid, by state law. And, for that matter, the part of the will giving you the property probably wouldn't hold up either."

"I understand this fully. You see, I don't have anything to help my argument of mineral rights ownership other than a gut feeling that something isn't right. Plus, I want to know what this company, Overshoot Mining, is up to. Are there significant minerals on this land? As you say, if the will in invalid, then everything's up for grabs, including who owns the land."

Wow! This could get complicated. Eric reached for his notebook as McDonnell talked. Unlike lawyers and their famed legal pads, Eric preferred the classic field book carried by geologists. He used two field books, one for his geological consulting business and one for his private detective work. "Don't mix business with pleasure!" was how he responded when asked about the dual field notebooks. But no one could ever pin him down about which of his occupations was business and which was pleasure! Was geology or private investigative work the pleasure? The answer was "Yes." This left his questioners scratching their heads.

Which notebook should I use for this case? I guess I'll use both; there're two sides to this investigation. "I'll need names, addresses, and phone numbers of your brother's family, neighbors, and friends who might remotely know anything about what was going on when your brother signed the will. I'll try to see what I can dig up from their memories. Now, about what the mining company might be after on the property? That'll require a different approach, but I'll see what I can do."

"Thanks, Mr. Bonfield. I hate ambiguity. This whole thing is a mess."

"Do you know anything about what's happening right now on the property? For example, are they drilling discovery holes or bulldozing land?"

"From what little I've learned; a lot of dozer work is pushing dirt around. They've cleared an area of bare rock. Blasting can be heard, so some rock might be removed. I don't know about any drilling."

Eric frowned. "That suggests they plan to do open pit work. Petroleum exploration or coal mining is unlikely in Magnet Cove. They must have some information about resources on the property or they wouldn't want the mineral rights. If they're after ordinary rock for construction, then an open pit quarry is likely. That hardly warrants secrecy. I can think of lots of other places where such rock is readily available and much nearer to known construction sites. Perhaps there's some sort of rare mineral found there; Magnet Cove is famous for these. The ones I'm familiar with could be extracted by either underground or open pit mining methods. My guess favors the open pit approach, which is much cheaper."

"Good thinking. I didn't know all that."

"It's hard to figure what's going on without visiting the site."

McDonnell nodded. "My sources don't tell me much. Overshoot Mining is very tight-lipped." He pulled out a printed sheet of paper with names of relatives and handed it to Eric. "Let me know what you find out." McDonnell picked up the check and a doggie bag with the remainder of his lunch. He strode quickly to the cash register.

Eric watched Sean McDonnell pay for their meals and exit the restaurant. *This man doesn't waste time with chit-chat! McDonnell knows what he wants and when he's got it, why bother with small talk?*

Curious, Eric stretched his neck and surveyed the parking lot. He was shocked to see McDonnell bypass the Jag and jump into an antiquated Chevy pickup, start the engine, and leave the lot. Eric pondered this choice of vehicle by an important businessperson in Arkansas's largest city.

While Eric mulled over McDonnell's strange choice of transportation, a well-dressed man rose from his table, went to the register, and paid his bill. Eric noticed the man took out his cell phone and pressed a button. Then he immediately pocketed the phone, quickly exited the building, and hurried to his pickup. *Must have started his vehicle remotely.* In another instant an explosion in the parking lot shattered windows of the restaurant, sending glass fragments over customers and their lunches.

The blast momentarily stunned Eric. After he gathered his thoughts and tried to clear his head, he stood, a bit wobbly, and surveyed the damage. Patrons staggered out of their seats. Some showed speckles of blood on their hands and faces. Everyone stared in disbelief through broken windows at the parking lot. The Jaguar had disintegrated into a flaming mass. Vehicles parked nearby felt the intense heat and suffered damage from flying fragments of the disaggregated Jag.

The man who pressed the button that apparently set off the bomb was driving fast out of the lot. Eric stumbled over broken glass and debris as he ran to the front door and watched as the black Toyota pickup careened from the lot. Eric reached for his pocket field glasses, but the vehicle turned a corner and he couldn't make out a license plate number. *Didn't look like an Arkansas tag.*

Eric called 911.

"Medical help and sheriff will be on the way."

He called the Hot Spring County sheriff's office directly with a description of the getaway unit. As a pickup aficionado, Eric knew the specific color, year, and model. After closing the connection, he turned to resurvey damage inside the restaurant. Eric tried to comfort guests spattered with blood until emergency assistance arrived. He'd been seated away from the window and got no more than a light shower of glass particles. *Thank God no one is seriously injured! But I've got a ringing in my ears.*

When sheriff deputies arrived, Eric gave them an account of what he remembered. "I got a decent look at the triggerman and can give a description to an artist at your crime lab. That might help catch the guy."

"Be a great idea. We got one of the best forensic artists in the state right here in Malvern. Y'all look her up and she'll do ya a great sketch."

"Thanks. I will."

EMTs tallied their business and found no customer with more than a few minor cuts, although all felt shaken. One person complained about not being able to eat their food and wanted a refund, while another fussed about missing an important appointment. *Join the crowd, folks!*

****

Eric's mind returned to the present chaos as he looked around at the emergency vehicles, stunned staff, and customers who stumbled out of the restaurant. Still gripping the door handle of his pickup, he inspected his vehicle for damage. *Glad I parked on the opposite side of the lot. My Ford just has dust from the explosion. Sheriff's deputies have all the information I can give. Time to drive to Malvern and see that artist.*

Chapter 2

As he bumped along one of the infamous Arkansas rural roads, Eric's mind wandered into more distant reminiscing.

****

Bombing of the Jag brings back memories of the Arkwell Oil Company case. That was the most dangerous P.I. work Joseph Hernandez and I ever survived. Earlier gigs were mild. The now famous Arkwell investigation catapulted Eric to near-national recognition and revolutionized his business. Almost overnight, Eric moved from a very good private detective to master sleuth. Prior to that blockbuster case, Eric ran a one-person consulting service solving geological problems and doing detective work on the side.

In the early days of his business, Eric did everything. After he became known for his expertise, Megan moved from part time to full time. She ran the office like a well-oiled machine. This allowed Eric to keep up with projects. Media exposure changed all that. The high profile take-down attracted both detective work and geological consulting. Eric found himself in high demand after his name was splashed on newspapers and TV interviews publicized his exploits. Eric couldn't hide. His odd combination of skills involving private investigation and geology drew people and organizations with complex problems. Requests for quotes poured into his tiny office. Eric felt overwhelmed.

Joseph Hernandez came on board during the Arkwell case and saved Eric's sanity and his bacon more than once. Joseph assumed much of the semi-technical work and Megan expertly outsourced as much routine work as possible. Their efforts allowed Eric to focus on more technical aspects of consulting and investigative projects. Joseph's experience in the oil patch, coupled with his keen mind, fearless attitude, and moral character matched Eric's business model.

Joseph had a knack for gathering field data and tackled detailed tasks with enthusiasm. Together, Eric and Joseph solved complex problems, bounced ideas off each other like ping pong balls, and became a powerful team. "Joseph," Eric said, "I've no idea how I'd ever survive without you. Two heads don't double efficiency, they quadruple it."

Joseph pushed such compliments aside, but inside he felt respected and appreciated. His wife, Sonya, became best friends with Eric's nearly-fiancé, Sarah Isaacs.

****

So much for the past. I've got to get to the sheriff's office while the image of the bomber is still in my head.

Malvern is the county seat of Hot Spring County and where the sheriff's folk hang out. Still losing glass fragments as he walked, Eric climbed the sheriff's office steps. He asked for the forensic artist.

A perky brunette popped out of nowhere and said, "That's be me! Hi, I'm Jackie."

"I'm Eric Bonfield, PI."

"Ah know who you are! Been the man who took down that gang over south of Little Rock, huh?"

"Very guilty, I'm sure. Right now, I'm here because one of your deputies said you're a fantastic artist who can generate a description I can give of the man who apparently blew up a Jaguar in the Highlands."

"Y'all set right down here and just tell me all 'bout this person."

After a lengthy description, Jackie said, "Y'all musta got a really good look at him."

"Sort of goes with my business, you might say."

She listened and continued sketching.

"His behavior was unique enough to catch my attention. He was one of the best dressed customers in the restaurant. Most folk were in work clothes."

"Ah knows the restaurant. Nice place, good food, and great place for dates." She winked at Eric.

He shifted uncomfortably but said nothing. After a few more touches, she asked Eric how close the sketch matched his memory.

"You nailed it! You're really good!"

"Blame the art school in Hot Springs. They specialize in trainin' us forensics."

"If your drawing is sent around the area, maybe this guy can be caught."

"Sure hope so." Jackie said this with another wink.

As he left the sheriff's building, Eric thought about how to explain what happened today to Sarah, Megan, and Joseph. His dusty pickup finally reached his apartment and jerked to a stop in its assigned space. He turned off the engine and sat for a moment, trying to arrange his thoughts. *What did happen? I had an interview with a new client. We agreed on a plan. Then the place blew up! What a way to start the day.* He pulled himself up the stairs and fought the impulse to lie down and take a nap.

After cleaning up and changing clothes, it was time to get back to work. After a stop at a car wash, he pulled his pickup into a parking space as close to his office as he could. *I'm not walking any farther than necessary. This morning was exhausting.*

He had just opened the office door when he heard Megan ask, "What happened at that restaurant in the Highlands?" Megan kept a sharp ear on police radio chatter and was full of questions about the explosion.

"Looked like I stepped into a battlefield. I'm afraid my new client may've been the bomb's target."

She peppered him with questions, which helped Eric better recall the events and led to various scenarios that might explain why there was a bomb and how it missed Sean McDonnell.

"Megan, your questions help me. I probably would've forgotten some important ideas if you hadn't bugged me." He jotted the ideas in his notebook. "I don't think we pay you enough."

Megan palmed him off but inwardly beamed. She enjoyed working in his office. Eric made her feel part of the investigative process. He and Joseph respected her, and she knew it.

Eric looked around. "Where's Joseph?"

"Oh, he's on that case about a missing child. Remember?"

"Oh, yeah. Any breaks yet?"

"Could be getting close, or so I last heard. Glad you're alright. Sorry about that Jag."

"Me too. I really think McDonnell was the target."

"Might be. Well, fun's fun, but I've got to get home. My husband'll be ravenous after his long plane ride from that New York convention. You called Sarah yet?"

"Just about to do that. She might be worried if she heard about the explosion." *Hope she hasn't eaten.*

She answered her cellphone. "Hi Eric. I hope you're calling about dinner. I'm famished."

"You read my mind."

"I've been working late on a brief for my boss's court case tomorrow. You caught me just in time. I'm ready for some serious food. By the way, how'd your lunch meeting with the new client go?"

"It was explosive!" said Eric. "And I mean that literally."

"What're you talking about?" Her voice shifted to a worried tone.

"Don't worry. I'm fine. Somebody's car blew up just after lunch. I'll tell you about it at dinner."

"Was somebody after you?"

"No, no. Nothing like that. I do have a concern that my new client might've been the target. I wonder if the bomber made a mistake and blew up the wrong car."

Sarah's voice shows tension. "Eric, what're you getting into?"

"I hope nothing. I'm probably off base. May have been a random event."

"Sounds like we need to talk about this 'new client' and "random event."

"Don't fret. This may all be just a couple of unconnected events." *I hope.*

"Humm. Let's hope so."

"See you at dinner." Eric appreciated Sarah's interest in his work. *I know men with spouses who could care less about what their husbands do. Sarah and I aren't engaged, but she keeps up on my work.*

Sarah and Eric's relationship wasn't ordinary. They were thrown together by dramatic events during the Arkwell Oil case. Death threats bonded them in a way neither Eric nor Sarah could fully explain. Without family to rely on, Sarah clung to Eric, and he willingly responded. Romance seemed inevitable.

After the Arkwell investigation concluded, they evaluated their connection. Common spiritual backgrounds cautioned them to take their time before advancing to engagement. The divorce rate in Arkansas mirrored the rest of the nation, and they didn't want to contribute to the data.

"We decided to date casually, but that's not easy to do," Eric shared with his parents. Their mutual attraction was powered by a chemistry neither could explain. When they were together, each found an emotional and spiritual connection. In the back of Eric's mind was Megan's favorite cautionary saying, "A solid relationship involves more than *chemistry*".

Sarah confided in a friend that she needed to get past the shivers she felt when Eric held her close. "I know a meaningful marriage needs a lot more than that." Their decision to let things develop slowly was difficult but they wanted to avoid hasty actions.

"What do you do on dates?" asked Joseph.

"Mostly we go out to eat, go to church, or see a movie. Spending too much time on Sarah's sofa is a temptation we try to avoid. An uncontrolled fire quickly burns up fuel."

He told another friend, "I want a marriage like Megan's. She and her husband enjoy each other's company but aren't joined at the hip."

Chapter 3

Eric picked up Sarah at her farm and drove to their favorite restaurant. At dinner they talked about the explosion. Sarah asked, "Why was the car bombed?"

"Got me. I'm puzzled by the whole affair. I called Sean McDonnell and told him what happened. He passed it off. The Jag wasn't his. Then I got to thinking about the timing of the explosion. It came too close to when McDonnell left the restaurant. I wonder if he was the target. Maybe we have an inept bomber who failed to check which vehicle McDonnell drove that day. But that doesn't make much sense; most professional bombers are more careful than that. Maybe this guy was a newbie and inexperienced."

"Have sheriff's officers located the pickup?"

"Not yet. I hope they find the guy before he leaves the area. His license plate was out-of-state."

During dessert, Eric's phone rang. He answered, listened for a minute, then hung up, and looked puzzled.

"Well?"

"They found a pickup that matched my description of the getaway Toyota truck. It was burned to a crisp on a remote road just across the line into Garland County. No sign of the driver."

"A lot of evidence up in smoke!" Sarah voiced Eric's thoughts before he could.

"Yeah. Now the only thing we have is my description of the bomber. I stopped by Malvern's forensics lab and Jackie, their artist, created a composite from my memory. She's really good."

"Is she pretty?"

Eric shook his head. "I suppose. She was kind of a flirt, but my eyes are on you."

Sarah blushed and apologized. "Sorry, but I'm a bit possessive." She smiled and gave him a wink more suggestive than Jackie's.

"Glad to hear it!"

As he was paying the bill, Eric's phone buzzed again. Another minute of listening and added puzzlement followed.

"What now?"

"A sheriff's deputy in Saline County to the east stopped a driver for speeding and gave him a warning ticket. He had an out-of-state license and seemed nervous. The officer let him go. An hour later the composite image created from my work with the forensic artist clicked with the deputy. He alerted headquarters."

"Did they catch him?"

"Nope. This guy could be anywhere by now. They've got an APB out with a last known location. Maybe they can locate the car with the deputy's description."

After Eric paid the waiter, they drove to her house. His phone interrupted their goodnight kiss. More listening, more puzzled looks.

"Well, tell me!"

"It seems that some official in Indiana recognized the sketch. This person is wanted in several states as a hit man for hire." Eric shook his head in disbelief. "Now things don't add up! A pro like him wouldn't make the mistake of rigging the wrong car."

"So, what do you do now?"

"Tomorrow I'm going to see Mr. McDonnell again. I'm not convinced this bomb is unrelated to him." After another attempt at a kiss, Eric succeeded and drove away.

Sarah watched his taillights disappear before closing her door. The faint hint of his cologne lingered in her memory. Her eyes sparkled as she thought of Eric.

The next morning Eric dropped in on Sean McDonnell at his office.

The businessman's assistant recognized Eric. "Ah know Mr. McDonnell will drop whatever he's doin' to hear any news y'all have." *Obviously from south Arkansas.* She knocked on her boss's door.

"Yes?" A deep voice resonated through the opaque glass.

"Y'all can go in now, Mr. Bonfield." She ushered Eric into a spacious but not opulent suite. As she held the door for him, Eric smiled. His mind continually analyzed the speech of anyone speaking to him. It was part of his investigative background. The diversity of accents in Arkansas usually identified most residents' home base. McDonnell's assistant was from well south of Little

Rock. On the other hand, Mr. McDonnell had long ago dropped any accent in favor of "business Midwest" expected of a person with his professional stature.

"Well, do you have anything for me?" McDonnell never beat around the bush.

"Yes, I do. Somebody torched the bomber's pickup. There must be some real money involved. That pickup was a brand-new Toyota and worth serious bucks. An identification based on my memory of the guy indicates he's a professional assassin. Such people don't make mistakes where they plant bombs, and the timing with respect to our meeting seems almost coordinated."

McDonnell looked shocked. "How do you think I'm involved with this bombing?"

"I don't know. It might be a random event unrelated to you. But, given that you're locking horns with a questionable company in a legal case, I wouldn't rule out anything right now. I'm wondering if this bombing somehow concerns you."

"Why me?"

"That's just the question I'm asking you. Is this mineral rights conflict such a serious matter that someone would try to blow up a Jag when we're talking about a legal case?"

"Not from my view! To me, it's a business situation with odd overtones. I can't think of anything that might push someone to kill me."

"Maybe it's the odd overtones that're involved." Eric observed.

"What do you mean?"

"I really don't know. Just speculating. But this bombing triggers questions I need to ask. What's most important right now? Is it the mineral rights or what Overshoot Mining is doing on the site? And what about safety concerns for you?"

McDonnell huffed. "Normally I can take care of myself. Let's not dwell on safety right now. The mineral rights problem is top drawer for me. I need all the evidence you can gather for my lawyers. What the company's doing on the property is important, but I'll leave it up to you to decide when you tackle that question."

Eric left Sean McDonnell's office and sat in his pickup, thinking. *I've got two things to work on. I'll need to divide and conquer. First thing is to interview Abe's relatives to see if they know anything about signing the will.*

To tackle the second question, I'll see what dirt Megan can dig up on the mining company." Eric smiled at his unintended pun. *If Overshoot Mining has any soiled laundry, our web-wizard Megan can find it.* He phoned and asked her to discover all she could about this company.

"I'm on it!" Megan said.

"If Overshoot Mining, Inc. has rotten apples in their basket, I need to know it, especially since attempted murder might be somehow involved." *Dirt or halos? She's got no equal in finding obscure data. Go, Megan, go!*

"Oh, and can you also find as much as possible about the criminal who set off the explosion? Anything you discover may be important."

"On it, boss!" She smiled. Searches were her specialty.

Now, face-to-face interviews. Eric's eye ran down the list of Abe McDonnell's relatives. *Might as well start with the one closest to Abe's farm. That'll be his nephew, Lewis.*

As he drove to Lewis McDonnell's home, Eric rehearsed what he learned from Sean. *Abe's wife died several years ago. No children. Most McDonnell family members don't move far from home base in the Highlands. This makes finding nieces and nephews easier.*

Eric's mind wandered. *I feel swamped with all the work piling up. Should I hire another geologist with a forensic background to handle the extra stuff?* He smiled. *How many private detective geologist types are out there? Would they fit in with our company values? And would that turn me into an administrator instead of working with people? Brrr. No appeal! Why give up what I love to do?* He shook his head and forgot about hiring anyone.

The Highlands were beautiful, in Eric's mind. Formed by dramatic geological processes ages ago, the rocks exposed by erosion told the story of their formation. Massive continental plates collided to deform otherwise flat-lying strata. Eric rehearsed these geologic events as he drove past outcroppings of rocks.

Suzie spoke from Eric's GPS. "Your destination is on the right."

"Thanks, Suzie," Eric said, with amusement. "You did it again."

Lewis McDonnell lived a short distance from Abe's farm. He was, by his admission, temporarily unemployed. Eric found him in a rocking chair on his front porch. "Hello Mr. McDonnell. I'm Eric Bonfield. Sean McDonnell hired me to investigate the death of your Uncle Abe."

"Well now! Thit be jist fine. Sit a spell and let's have us a talk." He pulled up a rickety wicker chair for Eric.

"Thanks. I know Abe's loss was a blow to the family. I don't like to discuss this, but Sean is concerned about the whole situation."

"Shore be strange!" began Lewis, as he chewed on a pipe with no tobacco in it.

"What's strange?"

"Thit thar whole thin' 'bout Abe and Sean, I mean."

"What thing?"

"Never did see them brothers as close. Related, ya know, but not much goin' 'tween 'em."

"What're you saying?"

"Sean and Abe? They war differ'nt. Sean, he a big shot in Little Rock. Abe, he run his farm; not much of a farm neither; had him some nice cows though. When we had us a broke engine or sumthin', we took it ta Abe. Fixed 'em up good, he did. Then them minin' guys come by and waved a contract in front o' his face."

"What can you tell me about Abe?"

"I warn't too chummy with neither Abe nor Sean, ya see. Abe? We lived right close, and we talked some. Him and his wife never had no kids. Guess thit be why they had lots o' folks over fir fun. Far as talkin' 'bout deep stuff, twarn't many folks Abe done thit with. Abe's closest kin, in talkin', ya know, that be my sis, Josephine, and her friend, Sophia."

"Why was that?"

"Josephine, she never put on no airs. Guess Abe liked thit. And Sophia, she always run with Josephine, so they seen Sean and his wife ever' so of'en. I ask'd Josephine 'bout Abe . . . what they talked 'bout. But all she done said was 'bout them bein' chummy, and he liked have'n 'em 'round."

I wonder why Abe didn't leave the farm to Josephine instead of Sean. "Any idea about Abe's will?"

"I heerd as how Sean got the farm. Scratched ma haid 'bout thit. Don't think Josephine got nothin'. 'Course, neither did none o' the rest o' us kin folk."

"What do you know about Overshoot Mining?"

"Odd folk! I heerd they got all them minin' rights. Quare, don't ya think?"

"It does seem strange. Any ideas why?"

"None on ma part. Might ask Josephine or Sophia."

"Have you ever had any dealings with the company or seen any mining on the farm?"

"Out ta the mine one time, 'tween jobs, ya know, and thought ta poke 'round and see what's goin' on. But, ya know what? Them guards war posted all 'round the mine. Took me a spell to convince 'em ta let me in."

"Did you discover anything while you were there?"

Lewis laughed. "'Fore they kicked me out, found a funny lookin' rock. Powerful heavy."

"Do you have it here?" Eric asked anxiously. Lewis went to the back porch. *Lewis's place looks like it might double as a "before" picture for a TV makeover. Doubt if it's been remodeled since it was built ages ago.* In a few minutes, Lewis emerged clutching a large black stone. Eric instantly recognized it as an iron-bearing rock. *Probably magnetite.* He took out his pocketknife, and the steel blade practically leaped to the rock.

Lewis was impressed. "Be that there what they call lodestone?"

"Yep. Its formal name is magnetite. Very few minerals are as magnetic as this one. Do you remember if there was a lot of this rock where you picked it up?"

"Jist a few lyin' 'round the mine. Them fellers didn't seem ta pay no mind 'bout it tho. Didn't care I took some."

"Did you see anything else that looked different?"

"Them guards didn't 'llow much time ta look 'round. They war mean lookin'. Didn't want ta git 'em riled up."

Eric puzzled over this observation. *Magnetite's a valuable iron ore but would need to be available in huge amounts to merit a mining operation.* Magnet Cove drew its name from the naturally magnetic mineral picked up in this small area. *Would Overshoot Mining be after magnetite? I don't believe it. Can't be enough here to afford the expense of mining such ore.* "Lewis, you're very helpful. Do you think your sister would mind if I talked with her about Sean's will?"

"Don't think she'd mind 'tall. We war all kinda surprised 'bout the will."

Eric asked Lewis if he would call Josephine and alert her that he'd like to visit.

"Shore can. Hope ya find out what's goin' on."

In his pickup, Eric mused over the contrast between Sean and Lewis McDonnell. Both had their cultural roots in the Arkansas Highlands, but that was where their similarity ended. Sean, from what Eric had learned online, moved out of his homeland early in life to attend the University of Arkansas and never looked back. He set his sights on a career in banking and purposely dropped the dialect of his forebearers. Apparently, Sean McDonnell believed this was important so he could fit in with others of his intended profession. This cultural separation was accelerated when his strong academic record allowed him to enter Harvard and earn an MBA.

Where do I fit in? I lack the dialect of earlier people in my family. Moving to Illinois to do graduate work affected me. Rubbing shoulders with international students required me to adopt a Midwestern speech pattern. They had a problem understanding my home talk. But I love to talk with all kinds of people! Lewis McDonnell brought back pleasant memories.

Better get back to today. He called Megan. "Any news on Overshoot Mining? I'm going to visit another of Sean McDonnell's relatives."

"Yes, but findings are puny. Not a big operation. Only mines are in Arkansas. They keep their work close to the chest. I'm surprised at the lack of information on the state's website about the company. I guess Arkansas must not pay much attention to small mining operations. I'd say Overshoot Mining is overlooked! But I'll keep looking." Megan chuckled.

Eric sighed. "The state is cash strapped. Oversight of small operators in several resource industries doesn't rank high on the priority list. Big name companies get most of the attention. Thanks, Megan. Looks like I'll have to do something else to see what's going on." He hung up.

I don't believe for a minute they're after magnetite. No way. There's got to be some other reason why they want mineral rights to Abe's property. This land grab must be about something else, but what?

He started his engine and paused. *Josephine McDonnell lives only a short distance away, but my pickup clock reads noon. My stomach says I'd better grab some lunch before I see her.* He called Josephine, introduced himself, and described his conversation with Lewis McDonnell. Lewis had beat him to Josephine's phone and cleared the way.

"Could I come and talk with you after lunch?"

"Be rite pleased. Do come." Josephine trusted Lewis.

Eric decided to visit the restaurant where the explosion took place. He was interested more out of curiosity than convenience. When he arrived, a cleanup crew had cleared remains of the Jaguar. An asphalt truck was beginning to repair the burned area. Café windows were temporarily covered with plywood. A sign read, "Open for business." Inside, a few customers were enjoying lunch. The floor was free of glass, and the interior looked only a little worse for wear. The same waiter who was at the cash register during the explosion came to Eric's table. "I'll have the special. How's the cleanup going?"

"Oh, guess comin' okay. I's here, ya know, when the blast took out the owner's Jag."

Eric blinked. "Oh, so it was the restaurant's owner's car?"

"Yep. Still don't know why somebody blasted it. Nice car, too!"

"Did the sheriff's people find anything?"

"Not much. But I seen the guy who run out the door right 'fore the blast. He took out in a hurry. Funny, he dropped a rock."

"A rock?"

"Yeah, I showed it ta the cops, but they didn't pay no mind."

"Look, I'm a private detective and sort of working on the case. Do you still have the rock?"

"Right here by the register. Want ta see it?"

"Please!"

The waiter brought the rock to Eric's table. A quick test with his knife verified the small black stone was magnetite!

"Whoa! Why'd the rock 'tach ta yir knife?"

"The mineral is magnetite. It's found in Magnet Cove and is a powerful natural magnet."

"Ain't never seen that 'fore. I heerd o' lodestone but never seen that knife trick!"

"Do you mind if I take this with me?"

"Nope. Don't do me no good."

"Thanks. Thanks a lot!" During lunch, Eric mulled over any connection between the small piece of magnetite and the guy who blew up the Jag. By the time lunch was over, Eric's face moved from hope to uncertainty. *Wait a minute! Why'm I excited about a bit of magnetite the thug dropped? It's a common thing around Magnet Cove. He could've picked it up at a souvenir shop instead of Abe's farm. May not be connected to Overshoot Mining at all.* His shoulders slumped as he walked to his pickup. *No use looking for fingerprints since the waiter handled it.*

Chapter 4

Eric brightened as he thought about interviewing Josephine McDonnell. *Maybe she'll have a clue about the unexpected bequests in Abe's will. I hope the interview won't take too long. I need to make it back in time to have dinner with Sarah.* Then Eric remembered he hadn't called her. He punched her number. She answered on the second ring.

"Hey, Sarah! How about dinner tonight at Frank's Pizza? I've some thoughts to share about the case I'm working on."

Her pause took longer than necessary. "So, you need a sounding board?" A bit of sarcasm dripped out of the phone.

Eric realized his faux pas. "Oh, I didn't mean it that way." He tried to reclaim the moment. "My main reason to call you is to hear your voice and ask if I can be with you. Anything else is strictly secondary." He waited to see how miffed she might be.

"Well . . . I'll accept your apology . . . but . . . pizza? Can't we go to Antonio's or someplace with an atmosphere that doesn't smell like burnt pepperoni?"

"You bet! Antonio's it is! How about six?"

"I'll be ready." She sounded fine at this point. Sarah almost choked, as she stifled a laugh. *I love to pull his string! I'll bet he's sweating!*

Eric mopped his forehead. Perspiration always marked stress in his life. *Why do I get so swept up in work that my personal life suffers?*

Josephine McDonnell lived in a remote back roads area not too far from her uncle Abe's farm. Her modest house needed paint, but the front porch was bedecked with brilliant flowers in pots that tried to cover some of the house's blemishes. *She must like flowers a lot more than exterior maintenance.* He knocked on the front screen door. It was secured by two hook-and-eye fasteners. After a couple of minutes, a slight, demure woman appeared. *Her straight, black hair could use a brush.* He introduced himself.

She acknowledged his phone call and, after eyeing him carefully, asked for identification. As he showed her his ID she said, "A body can't be too careful these days, ya know."

"I couldn't agree more."

Satisfied Eric wasn't a criminal, Josephine unlatched the screen door and ushered him into a modest living room. She waved her hand toward well-worn overstuffed chairs and a sofa. "Have a seat."

"Thanks. Ms. McDonnell . . ."

Josephine caught him in mid-sentence, "Jist stop right thar. Ma name be Josephine and I ain't no 'Ms'. Never been married. I don't put on no airs, so call me Josephine."

"Sorry about that." Eric caught himself; but it was too late to avoid a stern look. He didn't mean to comment on her marital status, but it came out that way. *What a way to start a conversation!*

After all, she must have good reasons for never marrying. "Please excuse me, Josephine. Let me start over. I understand you were very close to your uncle, Abe McDonnell. Is that correct?"

After a harrumph, she said, "Yep, me and him war real close. He told me stuff nobody ever knew 'cept me."

"That's very admirable. His brother Sean is concerned about the situation involving the will Abe left."

"Ah, now that there be a sure thing! We war all ponderin' how come Sean didn't get no mineral rights."

"Yes, that's Sean's concern too. Any thoughts on the subject?"

"I'd say it war somethin' relatable ta the agreement with them there minin' fellers."

"Did Abe ever talk with you about the will?"

"I knew'd Abe didn't hanker much fir them minin' men."

"Why would that be?"

"Guess'd he figgered they warn't on the up and up. Seems they kept changin' the percent Abe would git fir them minerals they dug up."

"But the will gave them mineral rights even though he didn't trust these guys?"

"Do seem funny, don't it?"

"Josephine, can you think back to the time when Abe signed the will? Did he act strange or anything like that?"

Josephine nodded. "I knows a lot 'bout that there subject. Ya see, I keeped a diary 'bout whatever goes on 'round here."

"Great. That might be very helpful. Do you mind if we take a look at it?"

"Not right now. Ya see, me and ma friend Sophia hid it real good. She knows all 'bout this stuff, ya see, cuz she war with me durin' all this minin' fracas . . . and, look here, I got ta go ta her house fir supper. It's gettin' on toward 5:30. How time do fly, don't it?"

Eric looked at his watch and realized he too would be late for his dinner date. Josephine's house was more than an hour drive to Sarah's farm. "Nice talking to you, Josephine. Mind if I come back after you find your diary?"

"No problem. What'd ya say yir name was?"

"Eric, Eric Bonfield. Thanks very much! Here's my card."

"It do say ya be a detective, don't it?"

"Yes, ma'am. I'll see you later then." He dashed to his pickup and almost threw gravel but didn't want to leave a bad impression on Josephine. He slowly exited her driveway.

On the way, Eric violated his personal code by calling Sarah while his vehicle was moving. "Sarah . . . I'm sorry . . . but I'm going to be a bit late . . . like maybe an hour late."

Sarah paused long enough to make a few beads of sweat appear on his forehead, "That's alright, Eric. I understand. Long interview, I suppose?"

"As a matter of fact, it was . . ." He caught himself and said, "I miss you!"

"Nice recovery, Eric!"

"No, really. I do miss you. You're the most caring person I know."

Sarah couldn't control her humor any longer. She laughed and said, "Eric, I love to make you sweat!"

The rivulets of perspiration stopped. Knowing that Sarah was pulling his leg, Eric relaxed and signed off. *Maybe the evening won't be tense after all!*

On the way to Sarah's farm, Eric tried to keep it under the speed limits. *No use.*

As he pulled onto her driveway, Eric remembered the shootout at Sarah's home when he killed a hired assassin who almost got the best of him. He never erased the memory of pulling the trigger. His gun released bullets which extinguished a life that night. His sense of the value of human life stepped aside as he defended Sarah and himself against an evil force bent on destroying them both. He'd never killed anyone before and that weighed heavily on his conscience.

He prayed many times for the family of the man he felled that evening. Until then, Eric never expected to draw his Glock in a lethal confrontation. The conflict in his brain returned whenever he faced dangerous situations. *I carry a gun for professional purposes. It's part of being a private investigator. Will I ever get over that dreadful night?* A discussion with his pastor helped but regret still lingered.

Sarah opened the door as he climbed the steps to her porch. She looked radiant in a blue and white dress. Her hair was done up in an eye-catching style. *Wow am I lucky or what!* "Hi, Beautiful! Waiting for someone who's usually late?"

"Maybe," she cooed. "Just thought I'd throw on an old thing in case anyone wandered by."

"Well, meet your wanderer!" He leaned over to give her a peck on the cheek.

Sarah reacted quickly and seized him by the neck and planted a gigantic kiss on his lips. "Just the wanderer I was waiting for," she purred.

He escorted her to his pickup, opened the door, and helped her into the seat as she eyed him mischievously. *Whew! This woman is something else!*

On the way to Antonio's, Eric and Sarah chatted about trivial things. Eventually she started talking about the efforts of the Arkansas EPA to clean up contaminated wells on her property. "What an awful task." The unscrupulous company that pumped nasty stuff down fake oil wells did a real number on the aquifer which provided water for several farms adjacent to hers. "Could this become another Superfund site? I've read about those. They cost a lot of money."

"I hope not; but it's likely. Taxpayer outlay to clean up the mess will be huge. I'm glad we could expose the bunch of gangsters. They left a real disaster for somebody else to take care of."

At Antonio's Eric finally felt it was okay to talk shop. "I've got a really odd situation," he said. "I think something weird is going on at Abe McDonnell's farm. That mine looks questionable to me."

"What makes you think that?" Sarah's sharp mind wanted details.

He told her about the magnetite from the mine and about the bomber who left in such a hurry that he dropped his piece of the mineral on the restaurant floor. "I can't believe that anyone would mine magnetite there. The relatives are all puzzled about the will in general and about the mineral rights being given to Overshoot Mining. I'm going to revisit Josephine McDonnell after she finds her diary. She recorded information about Abe and the mining company. She might have something to explain why Abe's will reads the way it does."

"Is she attractive?" asked Sarah.

"Oh, not too bad, I suppose," he said, deciding to play along.

Sarah slightly bristled. "Are these interviews chaperoned?"

"No, they're held in dim light at a romantic motel."

Sarah flushed, realizing he led her on. "Oh, Eric!"

"For your information, she's about the age of my mother, and further . . ." He looked into her hazel eyes and said, "I'm going with a wonderful woman with no competition."

At this Sarah dropped her eyes and then raised them. "Eric, you turn my heart upside down; do you know that?"

"Glad to hear it. I love upside-down hearts."

"I'm sorry if I seem possessive. It's just that I want to be the only one who stirs your heart. Jealousy isn't a virtue, but I don't want competition. Know what I mean?"

He nodded. Then their salads arrived, and Sarah said, "I wonder what our next step should be."

Eric thought a moment, laid down his fork, touched a napkin to his lips, and said, "Megan told me that before announcing their engagement, they took personality tests which were interpreted by a counselor. What would you think about taking such a test?"

"Megan's a wise person. I know you respect her a lot. I'm fine with that."

"Good. Would you mind checking to see what you can find?"

Sarah nodded. *At last, a breakthrough in this relationship standoff. Glad to move off dead center.*

After dessert, Eric took Sarah home. Following a lingering goodnight kiss, he said, "You are such a complete person, Sarah. You love God, you think about things so clearly, and . . ." inspecting her face he said, "you're beautiful."

Sarah felt a tingle all over as he spoke these words and held her close. "I . . . I am so happy to be in your arms, Eric. You're the most caring, thoughtful man I've known . . . .." Then she gave a mischievous grin and added, "Except for my father, my uncle, my cousin in California, and my . . ."

Eric caught the joke and tickled her. She sucked in air and wriggled away from his grasp. "And I love your humor," he said. They laughed together.

As Eric got in his pickup, she lingered on the porch and waved him off until his pickup disappeared out of sight. *What a man!*

Half-way to town, his mind was on Sarah when a bullet clipped the partially opened passenger's window and whizzed out the open driver's window. Fortunately for Eric, his stiff wide-brimmed hat cocked to the side deflected all but a small piece of glass that cut a gash across his chin.

The attack caught Eric so off guard that it took a moment to register what happened. He quickly did a flashback to an earlier attempt on his life. He swerved slightly as he reacted by stepping on the gas to get out of the assassin's line of sight.

What happened? Who shot at me? No time to figure it out. Death stalked him now. Another bullet broke the back window, was deflected by his gun rack before bouncing off a door post and ricocheting around the cab's interior. The bullet barely missed Eric's cheek. *This guy is good, but not good enough.* Eric's swerve and change of speed threw the shooter's aim off. The first bullet didn't miss by much. He might have leaned his head back while he thought of Sarah. *Maybe she saved my life!* Eric veered randomly over the road to further disturb the shooter. No more bullets struck the pickup. *Why doesn't this person blow out my tires and finish me off? Maybe bushes got in the way. Bad choice of location for an ambush; good choice for me. Thank you, Lord!*

Eric fumbled for his cell phone and speed dialed the Pulaski County sheriff's office. The officer on duty said a deputy was on patrol only a short distance away and would scout out the area. He added, "Eric, you know this getting-shot-at stuff is kind of old. Didn't this happen to you some other time?"

"Tell me about it," Eric replied. "I'm coming to the station to let you check for bullet recovery. I'm tired of this too."

The officer put out a call to look for suspicious vehicles in the vicinity.

Arriving at the station, Eric got out of his pickup shaking from the close call with a rifle bullet. Amy, a forensic expert, emerged from her lab. "Eric, are you alright? Your pickup doesn't look so good and neither do you."

"I've been better. It never feels good when somebody shoots at you."

"Here, sit down. I'll get you a drink." She went to a machine and brought him a coke.

"Thanks. Can you look over the cab and see if you can locate the bullet? Maybe that can help zero in on the shooter."

"First, let me give you some first aid. That scratch looks nasty."

Eric sat in a chair while Amy cleaned the wound and applied a bandage.

"Thanks. You're multi-skilled!"

"In forensics, ya got to be versatile! Now I'll look at your vehicle."

While Amy scoured the inside of Eric's pickup, Eric walked to the dispatch officer's desk. "Any luck yet?"

"Hold it! Just comin' in." He listened for a minute. "The deputy on patrol reported a car speedin' on a road near the attack site. He's givin' chase. Other officers just joined in the pursuit."

After a few minutes, another message arrived. "At a train crossin', the getaway car just made it across before a train blocked the sheriff's posse. They had a fair description of the car and plate number."

The desk deputy said, "I'll bet they find the car abandoned. The driver must've known the patrol car in front was close enough to see the license plate."

"Imagine you're right." Eric sighed. *I'll bet it matches the one with the APB.* Worried that Sarah might learn of the shooting incident before he told her, Eric called.

"Eric! What a pleasant surprise! Did our kiss not last long enough this evening?" She said this with a smile.

"I wish that's the reason for my call. Someone shot at me while I was driving home. Don't worry; I'm fine. Just a tiny scratch. No issue."

"What! Who shot at you? Are you sure you're all right?"

"Things are fine. My pickup will need new windows, but otherwise I'm in good condition. I didn't want you to find out from anybody but me."

Silence on the other end of the line was deafening. Finally, Sarah said, "So, is this another case like Arkwell? Are you in danger like before?"

"I wish I knew. Let me tell you this; I'll be on guard. You can be certain of that."

After a few more assurances, Eric closed the connection. He stared into the distance. *What've I gotten into this time!*

Returning to the dispatcher's desk, Eric learned that sheriff's deputies found a vehicle in a ditch five miles from the train crossing. It matched the description. No sign of the driver. *License is the same as the APB.* Eric stayed at the station and listened to radio talk. Passing the time, Eric asked the desk deputy if he knew anything about the Overshoot Mine on Abe McDonnell's place. *They've got to be the people shooting at me!*

The deputy laughed and put down his coffee cup. "You bet! That place is guarded like a high security prison. You'd think they're minin' gold or platinum. I was on a team searchin' for a prison escapee and traced him to the area 'round the mine. We asked the guards for permission to search the mine. They put up quite a fuss 'bout us goin' on the property."

"Ever get inside the mine?"

"We finally pulled authority and searched Abe's farm. I argued with the guard for a long time before I got permission to look around the mine."

"What'd you see?"

"That's what's funny. Lots of usual earth movin' equipment you'd expect to see. But it all sat idle. Dirt and rocks in piles 'round a large pit. While I snooped around, lookin' for our suspect, a minin' truck arrived and the guard stopped him. All the time I looked for the robber, the driver just sat in his truck. It's like he was waitin' for me to leave. Maybe I'm paranoid but that's what it felt like. After I couldn't find the escapee, I thanked the guard and left."

The deputy's story piqued Eric's interest. *Maybe the lingering truck held a clue.* "Did you see any name on the side of the truck?"

"Nope. Seemed strange. Usually those vehicles got some company name on the side, so you know they're legit."

Eric agreed. "Anything else you noticed?"

"Yep. Why weren't they diggin' in mid-mornin'? I've been to other mines with ore piles but didn't see any on Abe's place. All was rocks and dirt. And no ore processin' equipment neither. All kind of strange."

Amy came by the desk and said, "Eric, I found a bullet in the cab. Don't know if we can match it with a rifle but we'll try."

"Good news, Amy. I appreciate your work."

"We'll need to keep your truck so we can go over it in detail. Then we'll let the insurance company have their turn. Sorry to tie you up."

"Understood. I'll see if anybody is going off shift and can give me a lift to a late-night rental."

"I can do it. Off in 10 minutes." The desk deputy said this obligingly.

Chatting on the way to find a rental, the deputy said, "Eric, you're one lucky guy! I've never known anybody to dodge more bullets than you."

"Well, I don't call it luck. I'm thankful to survive. God is good."

"Guess so."

The rental agency was open late for such people as Eric who found themselves without wheels.

"Mr. Bonfield! Haven't seen you for a spell. Your pickup on the mend?"

"Afraid so. Somebody's bullets took out a couple windows."

"Got just the car for you, complete with remote starter, as you usually require."

A sedan! Groan. Part of being a PI, I guess.

Arriving at his apartment, Eric's mind lingered on Sarah's reaction to his danger. *How do I help her with this?* Not thinking of an answer to his own question, he decided to concentrate on the case. *Criminal activity at the mine might be real, but what kind? Why'd the truck wait during the deputy's search? Was it hauling stuff in or taking something out? Why no mining activity and no ore processing equipment?* Scenarios began to build in Eric's mind. Sleep was difficult that night.

Chapter 5

The phone rang before Eric's alarm did. He snapped awake and fumbled for his cell. Eric listened intently with a creeping sense of understanding.

"This is Amy in forensics. We've matched the fingerprints on the steering wheel of the abandoned assassin's car with the person police identified as the bomber of the Jag. Your sketch sealed the deal. And, of course, the license plate matched the guy a deputy stopped too."

"Thanks, Amy. He must've been in a hurry to escape and didn't wipe the car down. Professional killers don't usually make that mistake. It must be the same guy who blew up the café owner's car who shot at me last night. This makes me wonder what the connection is between the restaurant owner and me. Why target us both?"

"Ya got me! That's your job!" Amy gave a measured chuckle and signed off.

It's looking more and more like this leads to Sean McDonnell. After all, we were talking at the restaurant. How'd he know Sean wanted to put me on the trail of Overshoot Mining? Do they have a phone tap, or did the killer have a listening device to hear our conversation? Did he trail Sean or me to our meeting? Too many questions!

Eric cleared the sleep from his mind as he tried to make sense of Amy's findings. *The bomb can't be some random attack on the restaurant owner. I wonder if the restaurant owner and McDonnell are tied together. Since the killer muffed his attempt on my life, I wonder how his employer feels about him. Must be upset. This case is much bigger than Sean McDonnell could have imagined.* Danger and death lurk close by. *McDonnell must be warned!*

Eric quickly dressed and dashed to his rental car. He missed that pickup. *Driving a sedan is boring, but it gets me from point A to point B.* He sighed and drove to McDonnell's office. *I'll bet Sean is an early-to-work person.* Eric guessed right; no secretary guarded Sean's unlocked door.

Eric knocked and McDonnell's gruff voice boomed, "Come in."

Glad not to see a corpse, Eric entered. "Mr. McDonnell, I've got some important stuff to share." He told Sean about the deputy's visit to the mine, the attempt on his own life, and the identity of the assassin who must have torched the Jaguar and shot at Eric. "I think there's a definite connection with all this and the purpose of our meeting at the café."

McDonnell sat stunned. "So, you think somebody at Overshoot Mining is behind what you've described?"

"If Overshoot isn't involved in some way, then this is the weirdest set of circumstances. The bomber either picked the wrong vehicle or was after the restaurant owner. But I don't think this was a case of mistaken identity. Professional killers like this guy don't usually make such mistakes. I was targeted because I ate lunch with you at the restaurant. Overshoot must be in back of these events. I fear for your life, sir."

Sean McDonnell set his jaw and said, "If all you say is true and I'm in danger, what do you recommend?" His matter-of-fact approach to problems cut to the chase.

"Be very cautious. Skip any routines you usually follow during the day. Exit by different doors from the building. Randomly use a taxi or have someone you trust pick you up. Don't drive your pickup, but if you do, put it in a secure place where it can be watched. Take different routes to get home. I assume you have security at your house. Increase it if you can." Eric paused before proceeding cautiously, "And I think you might want to consider locking your office door."

McDonnell scowled but scribbled notes as he bit his lip. "Good advice. But this goes against my nature; you should know that, Eric. However, I'll try to be cautious. What're you going to do?"

"I must see Josephine right away. If she's got incriminating evidence in her diary, then I'm fearful she might be a target if Overshoot knows about it. She should probably move somewhere safe until this blows over."

"I'll provide for her in any way I can," said McDonnell.

Eric left Sean's office. He'd parked in a place difficult for someone to mess with his car. Just to be safe, he walked around the car and checked the usual places a bomb might be placed by some casual passerby. Sure enough, a small device sat magnetized to the left front tire well. He ran from the car and speed-dialed Little Rock police. Barely far enough from the car to avoid death, Eric felt a blast as the remotely triggered device sent pieces of the vehicle in all directions. A fragment of shredded plastic ripped through the back of his jacket and cut a groove in his shoulder. Sean McDonnell came running out of his building to see what happened. Eric shouted, "Get back inside!"

Eric worried the bomb might be a decoy to draw McDonnell into the open where a killer could shoot him. Police arrived in a few minutes and secured the area. They took Eric's testimony and searched for clues. EMT personnel asked Eric if he wanted transport to the hospital.

"No, thanks. Just clean up that cut if you don't mind."

Sean McDonnell cautiously exited the bank and found Eric receiving a bandage. "Are you hurt?"

"Just a scratch. Whoever did this is serious about harming me."

"I don't like putting you in danger. What can we do?"

"It goes with the territory. Fortunately, I found the bomb before it went off. I'll need to be careful. Now that they have my attention, I want to catch whoever's behind this."

With a sigh, McDonnell shook his head and returned to the bank.

Eric turned to a police officer and asked, "Could you drop me off at my car rental?"

"No problem. Glad to help. Looks like you won't be driving this one."

Eric's presence at the car rental office sent groans rippling through the agency. He rarely returned vehicles in good condition. "Can I have another one?" he asked timidly. Reluctantly they gave him a car. "Does this one have a remote starter?"

"Yes, that's the only kind we'll give you!"

Eric smiled and thanked the agent.

Got to get to Josephine McDonnell's place right away. She might be in danger. He called Josephine's phone. No answer. Eric's heart began to pound.

He called her friend Sophia. Josephine had given him Sophia's phone number in case he wanted to talk with her. She answered on the second ring. After explaining who he was, she responded, "Oh, yeah. Josephine told me 'bout you. She should be home."

"I called but got no answer."

"Strange. She picks up quick. Never knew her ta not answer a phone."

Eric asked if Josephine told her about the diary.

"Yep. I knows all 'bout that there diary. Mighty good notes Josephine takes, she does. And I knows where it's hid too."

Eric thanked Sophia. "I'd like to talk with you further, if I could."

"That'd be jist fine. Come when ya like."

Eric signed off and drove toward Josephine's in a hurry. The hour gave him time to work through possible explanations for recent events. *The bomb on my car convinces me Overshoot is concerned I'll find something that harms their case in court. Right now, I don't have any evidence against them. It's all circumstantial. This bomb attempt will worry Sarah. She expects me to be safe. Wish I could control that!*

He called Sarah's phone. It went to voicemail. "Hi Sarah. Just so you know, somebody blew up my car. I only have a scratch.

Don't worry. I'm being careful. Love ya." *No clue how she'll handle this news.*

Eric prayed for Josephine's safety. *I've a hunch the thug who tried to kill me won't stop until all persons who know something about this case are silent. But I don't know who else is in danger! And if I did, how could I warn them?*

Josephine's house finally came into his line of sight. As Eric got out of his rental car, an eerie feeling crept over him; things were too quiet. The dog that greeted him earlier didn't occupy a seat on the porch. Eric jumped the steps and pounded on the door. It stood ajar. He shouted, "Josephine!" No answer. He drew the Glock from his jacket, carefully opened the door, and stepped gingerly across the threshold while keeping alert for danger. Nothing. The deathly silence was slightly marred by a gentle groan that came from the kitchen. He rushed there. On the floor, in a pool of blood, lay Josephine.

Eric called 911. He knelt by Josephine and examined her wounds. Several bullet holes marred her body. None of the shots seemed lethal. *Whoever did this was clumsy or in a hurry.* No major organ areas showed damage. Eric grabbed dish towels and applied tourniquets to her arms and a leg where blood oozed out. He knew enough first aid to do this carefully. *Come on, ambulance!*

"Josephine, can you hear me? This is Eric Bonfield. I'm here to help. An ambulance is on the way." Her eyes fluttered but didn't stay open. "Stay with me, Josephine. You can make it!" He kept talking, trying to keep her alert enough to prevent shock from taking over her body. Even with some blood loss, Josephine remained semi-conscious. "Talk to me, Josephine. Who did this?"

Her eyes opened enough to stare into Eric's face, and she tried to speak. Her words came with difficulty. "I . . . I . . . never saw 'fore . . . he ask'd 'bout . . . mine . . . contract . . . Abe." At this she coughed, and her eyes closed momentarily.

"Did you tell him anything?"

Her eyes fluttered opened again. "Told him . . . leave . . . not sayin' nuthin' . . . he shoots . . ."

He focused on keeping Josephine alive until EMT personnel arrived. Eric glanced around the house. It was a mess. Furniture lay on its side. Magazines and books were scattered on the floor. The place was ransacked. "Hang with me, Josephine." Finally, he heard the wail of the ambulance. "Medical people are coming to help you, Josephine."

EMTs dashed in the door and moved to stabilize Josephine before carrying her to their vehicle. Eric's call to the Hot Spring County sheriff's office requested an escort for the ambulance and a guard at the hospital. One of the drivers looked at the place and said, "Wonder what they was after here?" Eric didn't respond but thanked them for coming quickly.

As the ambulance left, Eric's mind skipped to Sophia. *She might be in danger too!* He called and told her about Josephine. "Don't admit anyone except me or a sheriff's deputy." He phoned for more help from the sheriff's office in Malvern and drove quickly to Sophia's. It wasn't far, but he didn't take any chances. He kept looking over his shoulder. *Got to have backup. Too big for one person.*

As he drove, Eric prayed for Josephine's recovery and the safety of Sophia. Approaching Sophia's house, things looked normal. A couple of dogs lounged outside and barked routinely before returning to their rugs on the porch. He parked and, amid fainting dog noise, approached the porch. He knocked and identified himself. The door slowly opened, and a wide-eyed

Sophia stared at him. He showed his identification and she let him in.

"Sophia, I'm glad you're okay. Has anyone been here?"

Sophia's body visibly shook as she said, "Yeah! Black car come by 'fore ya called. He wanted ta talk 'bout Josephine. Didn't like his looks, so's I said come back later an' locked the door. He left. I been scared to death!"

And rightly so. He explained the attempted murder of Josephine. "But she's in good hands now. Given her condition, they'll take her to a Little Rock hospital. She lost some blood but EMTs said none of the wounds seemed life-threatening. I'm so glad you didn't let that man in your house. You did the right thing."

Sophia collapsed in a heap onto a dilapidated overstuffed chair and began to sob. Eric tried to console her.

"I keeps a shotgun by the door an' told that dude I didn't hanker no strangers 'round my place. Thit war 'nough fir him, I guess."

A sheriff's deputy car pulled up to the house. "I called for help, just in case." He asked the deputy to park a distance from the house and keep an eye out for a black car.

Sophia took a deep breath and exhaled. "What'd that guy want, anyways?"

"I think they want to know if anyone knows something about Abe McDonnell's will and the Overshoot Mining Company. That's about all I can say right now."

"If anybody know'd 'bout them things, Josephine an' me, we'd be the ones, that's fir sure. Josephine, she took good notes. An' me, well, I listen good."

"Sophia, you said earlier that you know where we can find Josephine's diary; is that right? It might have the clues we need."

"Yep, I kin take ya right there."

Eric explained to the officer about the general situation and suggested both Sophia's and Josephine's houses be surveilled in case anyone in a black car returned. The deputy radioed for more help and moved further down the road.

Sophia and Eric drove to Josephine's place. By the time they arrived, sheriff's deputies were combing the grounds for any identifying signs. From tire tracks and Sophia's general description of the car, they put out an alert. The situation was out of hand, so the sheriff in Malvern contacted law enforcement officers in several counties. The layout of county boundaries in the vicinity of Magnet Cove brings several close together. Jurisdiction could fall into any one of them depending on the exact location of an incident. Cooperation was part of the law enforcement culture in the adjoining counties.

Sophia led Eric to an old garage. A broken lock lay by the open door. Crammed to the ceiling with junk, the building showed the assailant's failed attempts to find the precious diary. Eric shook his head as he surveyed the debris. *Junk is a relative term. Might be treasure waiting to be discovered.*

Ignoring the jumble of stuff, Sophia went to what seemed to be a makeshift wall board. She reached around a two-by-six and pulled out a battered book, the diary! "Here 'tis!" she announced triumphantly. "Thit thar jerk don't know nuthin' 'bout where we hide stuff."

"Sophia, you're a genius and a gem! Do you know about when the contract and the will were signed? I'm especially interested how close these signings were to Abe's death."

"Shore do!" And she rattled off dates from memory. Eric began writing frantically in his field book to keep up with her rapid-fire details.

"Sophia, can we go back to your house and go over this diary together?"

"Be right pleased."

When they returned to Sophia's, Eric pulled his car around back—hopefully out of sight. They settled around her kitchen table while a deputy positioned his patrol car in a concealed location between the two women's houses. He couldn't see either house but was about half-way between them. His backup was stationed at Josephine's.

Sophia could read Josephine's handwriting better than Eric and knew just where each entry was located and its date. An invaluable source of facts, she added juicy items to the text. Eric's hand flew as he took notes. He wished for a small computer to type all the information gathered from the diary and Sophia's memory. Her frequent pauses allowed him to follow most of the tale.

A story evolved. Abe, Josephine, and Sophia all doubted the sincerity of the first Overshoot representative. This guy promised the Moon. After he left, they conferred, and all agreed something didn't add up.

I wonder what made Abe change his mind, so he eventually signed the contract? The second visit involved the company's CEO. He seemed more believable and Abe began to relax. Still, questions remained.

Succeeding visits involved a lawyer and somebody else. Sophia didn't remember what his title was. As the visits piled up, the company talked with Abe at a distant location, apparently to be away from Josephine and Sophia. The ladies bombarded Abe with questions after such meetings. He resented their intrusion into his business affairs. Abe seemed to soften in the face of Overshoot's barrage, although Josephine and Sophia weren't convinced that everything was fine. They warned Abe to read the contract very carefully and not be in a hurry to sign.

Fewer and fewer visits were held at Abe's home. This kept Josephine and Sophia out of the picture. The Overshoot crowd would arrive unannounced and quickly take Abe away from his farm. This way, the cadre of critics weren't around to heckle the shysters. Eventually, Abe felt worn down. His health deteriorated as the talks continued. Josephine worried about him and tried to get Abe to see a doctor. A stubborn man, Abe distrusted physicians. "They're jist after yir money," he said.

Josephine's concern focused on the smooth-talking company lawyer. Abe became more vulnerable as his health went downhill. The contract was apparently signed without the presence of Abe's family or friends.

Work began immediately at the mine site. Equipment moved in. Trees were removed. Soil was peeled off and rock blasting began. Josephine and Sophia were both dismayed.

Then the lawyer asked Abe about his will. Abe said it was written before his wife died. The Overshoot attorney just happened to be an expert on wills and was certain the will should be changed. He would be glad to help. Abe, in his weakened condition, eventually signed the revision.

Josephine and Sophia were very upset because Abe, even in his confused state of mind, made a new will. The duo demanded to read it, but Abe stubbornly refused, not wanting anyone messing with his business deals. His rapidly failing health worried both women.

The company representatives had picked up the skepticism of Abe's niece and her friend at an early stage. They did everything possible to visit Abe only when the ladies played cards at a neighbor's house or were otherwise absent. Most of the company representatives met with Abe at a restaurant. Sophia and Josephine also missed the signing of the new will. This was done at the farm not long before Abe died. The women were convinced Abe was in no condition physically or mentally to sign anything.

Reluctantly, Abe saw a doctor before signing but didn't tell his niece. Ink had dried on the legal documents before she knew about the will. Josephine and Sophia never saw either the contract or the revised will. The company's attorney conveniently put the documents in a safe deposit box with only Abe's name on the admitting card. *What a perfect setup for illegal activity. It was well-orchestrated by a crooked lawyer.*

The diary told an even more interesting story about the situation surrounding Abe's death. A caregiver stood at his bedside day and night. Josephine visited often with Sophia in tow. As the end neared, Abe began to talk about the will and contract. He regretted signing either but thought it was of no use trying to change them. "Everybody'd say I war too feeble to make good decisions."

The lawyer conveniently made himself medical power of attorney and executor of the estate. As a last desperate measure, Abe rallied and scrawled a note in Josephine's diary renouncing the contract and the will. He wanted the original will to be the correct one. He signed it shortly before he passed away. Josephine and Sophia both signed as witnesses. None of them supposed this made any difference legally, but they decided to keep it just in case. Eric's eyes widened when he read the scrawled note. Fortunately, Abe also scribbled the date he signed the replacement. But no notary was present to verify the signature. Eric smiled.

In Arkansas, I know that a notary is not necessary for a will to be valid. A person must be of sound mind and not coerced for the will to be in force. Witnesses need to attest to the state of the person's mind at signing. In the case of last-minute wills without a notary, the witnesses need to go to the Register of Wills to verify the authenticity of Abe's signature. But one is in the hospital. Sophia must be kept safe to reverse the fake will produced by Overshoot Mining.

Eric asked about the old will. "Do you have a copy of it?"

"Thit thar lawyer took the original old will with 'im. But, ya see, he didn't know thit Josephine made a copy o' it an' keeped it in a safe place. Only me and her know'd where." Eric suggested they place it in a safe deposit box with access by several relatives. Sophia knew Josephine would agree. "I kin git thit old will, if'n ya like?"

"That would be great."

Sophia walked to one of closets, picked up a rusty screwdriver stuffed in an old pair of jeans, and pried up a board below some dresses. She fished out a rolled paper and handed it to Eric. "Here it be! We keep stuff well hid."

They had exhausted the diary's contents just as Eric heard a car pull in Sophia's driveway. He looked out the front window. Sure enough, tires of a black car kicked up dust. A burley man got out. Eric quickly called the deputy on stakeout. The deputy had seen the car slowly cruise by his position. He called for backup that waited at Josephine's house.

Eric told Sophia to go to the door and ask him what he wanted. Eric drew his Glock. Sophia cocked the shotgun she kept near the door. "Can I come in?" the man asked. "I just want to ask you some questions about your friend Josephine."

"What's ya want ta know?" she asked through the door.

"Just some friendly conversation. I'm from the company that has the mine on her uncle's old property. Just want to see what you know about it."

"Ain't talkin'."

"Sorry to hear that," said the speaker and Eric saw him draw a gun. Eric motioned for Sophia to move away from the door and to the side, out of view from the front windows. The man shot into the door hoping to catch Sophia off guard. Then he kicked in the flimsy wood structure. It flew off its hinges. In the next second, the man burst through the door only to be met by shotgun blasts from Sophia's weapon. She wielded a double barrel 12-gauge model. Sophia knew how to handle a gun. She downed the thug before he barely entered the room.

Eric had intended to disarm and arrest this person for questioning. But Sophia's intention of defending her property against intruders who shot at her preempted Eric's plans. From Sophia's point of view, she didn't truck with no trespassers! The man collapsed as blood poured from gaping wounds. The shock on his face spoke of surprised death.

Eric rushed to the man, but his eyes showed nothing but frozen, blank terror. The sheriff's deputy, who just arrived, had also hoped to get the drop on the shooter, but Sophia's quick action put a stop to that plan too. There would be no interrogation and no confession to tell who the contact with the company might be. A witness who might finger the mastermind behind these attacks departed this life too quickly to retrieve any information. Eric hated to see even violent criminals put to death. He offered a silent prayer. He and the deputy agreed this was self-defense, and Sophia stood well within her rights.

Sophia put down her weapon and collapsed in her easy chair. She had a blank look on her face. "What'd he hafta go an' bust in like thit fir? If'n he'd ask'd nice, I mita 'lowed him ta talk."

Eric tried to comfort Sophia as best he could. She stayed seated and mumbled about "them city criminals".

Soon the Hot Spring County sheriff showed up for the event. He shook his head and said to Eric, "Man, you seem to be 'round when things get excitin'! I've heard 'bout you from folks in Pulaski County. You keep the sheriff busy over there too!"

Eric didn't have a comeback for this comment because of its painful accuracy. "I wish I didn't have to be involved in this and other messes, but here I am."

Forensic specialists poured over the black sedan, gathering as much information as they could. Unfortunately, documents identified it as a rental with no valuable clues. It was paid for in cash. No cell phone was found. *Fingerprints verified what I assumed from my memory of the man at the restaurant, that this was the criminal who shot at me, blew up two cars, shot Josephine, and was wanted in other states as a murder-for-hire contract employee. What a resume! And what did it get him?*

Everyone involved in this case must keep on their toes. That includes me. He turned to the sheriff and said, "With so little success, except for badly wounding one relative, the price on the heads of all targeted parties in this case must be going up. Everyone better be on watch!"

Then he froze. *Sarah! I was at her house. These people must know about our relationship.* Almost in a panic, he phoned her. No answer.

Not again! She experienced kidnapping twice in the Arkwell Oil case. *Would this group of clowns do the same?* Excusing himself from Sophia and the sheriff's people, he said, "I've got to see if Sarah's okay. Can you see about repairing this door and protecting Sophia so she's safe; she's a key witness in this case?" He also left instructions with the sheriff for safe storage of the diary and a copy of the old will.

I wonder if Sean McDonnell is next on the hit list. I hope he's taking the precautions we discussed. Eric again broke his own code by phoning while driving. Under normal circumstances he always pulled to the side of the road to make or receive a cell phone call. *No time for that now.* He pushed well past the speed limit to reach Sarah's house. *She should be off work by now and arriving home soon. We didn't make arrangements to get together tonight, so she could be anywhere.*

Unfortunately, Sarah's cell phone carrier had several dead zones between the city and her home. Eric convinced her to keep her separate GPS locater on, as a safeguard. Right now, Eric drove through his own dead spot; the phone sat useless in its carrier. *Everyone I know uses hands-free cell phones in their vehicles. I've never been convinced of the safety of such technology, especially for me. I get too distracted to drive safely when I'm on a phone call. So, what am I doing now?*

He worried, but he also prayed. As he drove, Eric also talked aloud to himself: "How do I get mixed up in such complicated and dangerous assignments? I'm just an ordinary consulting geologist who happens to like private detective work. I get a thrill out of solving difficult geological problems and crime cases. After all, they're a lot alike. I study a past event and try to find what happened. I keep all options open and don't assume anything until there's solid data." Talking kept his mind off what might be happening at Sarah's farm.

"I need to talk with Sean McDonnell and let him know about the 'real' last will. Sean's attorneys can wade through the details and see if the handwritten note supersedes the contrived will and contract. My job? To gather evidence and help police find people to arrest. So far, only a dead body is available; Sophia made certain of that. She did her job in self-defense. Now we've got to keep her safe to help verify Abe's signature on the scrawled will in Josephine's diary."

Eric kicked himself for exposing Sarah to such dangerous people. *The stuff I fall into.* He never doubted Sarah's strength as a person; she can handle almost any situation. *But these people I'm dealing with are violent.*

His shoulder gash began to throb. *Better get this checked out. No time to do it now.*

As Sarah's house came in sight, Eric looked anxiously for her car. In the darkening evening hour, shadows spread across the farm. He saw no evidence of her vehicle. Eric's heart rate increased. He pulled in front of her house and jumped out. His knock at the door yielded nothing.

Sarah gave him a key early in the Arkwell Oil case, and now he used it. Carefully entering so he didn't disturb any evidence, he looked around for signs of a struggle. Everything seemed to be in place, but his eye caught something. A dusty footprint left a barely distinguishable image on the hardwood floor. Eric tensed and drew his Glock. The print belonged to a man not a woman. *Better try a trick to be certain.* He cleared his throat and said, "Sarah? Are you here?"

Chapter 6

Clouds prevented moonlight from illuminating much of the hallway leading to Sarah's bedroom. In the dim light, Eric stepped quickly to the side just as a man appeared in the bedroom doorway and fired in the direction of his voice. *What I expected.* Crouching low, he fired at the center of the doorway in hopes of finding the man's outline. A grunt and then the sound of a person slumping to the floor followed. *Is this guy shot or bluffing? Like I trust that falling sound! Probably a fake to draw me out.* Eric waited. Seconds passed.

He grabbed a pillow and tossed it into the open hallway. It drew a bullet. Eric timed his shot so he could fire the instant he heard his opponent's weapon discharge. This time a scream shattered the silent house; thrashing on the floor was accompanied by coughing. Then it grew strangely quiet. *I'll try another ruse.* He stomped his foot and threw another pillow. No reaction. He shouted, "Do you give up?" Silence.

Cautiously, Eric rose and lightly stepped toward the hallway. He chanced a peek around the corner and drew back. Another bullet ripped wood from the wall. Eric fired again, and this time he heard a noise of metal clattering on the wood floor, and a clearly distinguishable gurgle. He looked again. A man lay sprawled on the floor with a gun at his side. Keeping the gunman covered, Eric moved forward. He kicked the gun out of the way and knelt beside the downed man. Eric touched the criminal's neck. *Weak pulse. Will I ever catch a witness to question?*

Is this the only person in the house? Can't drop my guard. Eric silently moved back into the living room and waited. He heard the faintest sound of a footfall. *Somebody else here!* This movement also came from Sarah's bedroom. *Got to be careful. It might be Sarah or somebody holding her hostage. Doubt she's here though. Her car isn't around. But they could've taken it and her someplace else. Or maybe she isn't home, and they just waited for me to show up.*

Darkness enveloped the house. *This second person might suddenly jump out, assuming I'm still kneeling by the downed man.* Eric stood at the edge of the junction of the hallway and the living room. His ears again picked up the faint sound of a footfall. It was barely discernible.

Glock at the ready, he waited. Then he saw a figure step into the doorway and fire at the assumed place where Eric would be kneeling. Eric fired but he apparently only nicked the assailant. The shooter fired in Eric's direction. Bits of wood scattered over the hallway. Eric fired again. His bullet found its mark. A gun dropped and the person collapsed to the floor. Eric carefully moved into the hallway. *Hope this guy is still breathing.*

"Are you alive?" It seemed like an odd question to ask, but he had to know. No answer. "Who do you work for?" Still no response. Eric paused long enough to reload his Glock. No telling how many more rounds he might use tonight. Eric advanced to the second man. The gunman's breath came and went with irregularity. *Still alive.*

Eric didn't trust that he'd taken down all guilty parties. He stole a glance around the corner of the bedroom. Incredibly, a bullet tore into the wood paneling and grazed Eric's shoulder. The shot caused him to wince from the pain, but he was able to fire around the corner. No answering shot. *How many are there? Their employers really want me dead.*

Another stolen glance around the corner. Another answering bullet. Eric fired again. A hoarse cough, gagging, a clatter of a gun on the floor, and a body dropping. Eric leaped into the bedroom to find another man gasping for breath. "Who hired you," Eric demanded.

"I don't wanna die . . . I'm just a hired gun . . . Jimmie . . . he hired us."

"Jimmie who?"

This third man didn't answer. He lost consciousness. Eric went to the third downed man. He was alive but in shock. Eric surveyed the carnage. He didn't know if he'd just sent one man to eternity and left two others in serious condition or if all three would live. *What a mess!* Eric called the Pulaski County sheriff's office and requested multiple ambulances and deputies.

Eric went to each man and checked their breathing. He administered emergency first aid to stop the bleeding. As he did, Eric prayed aloud they would survive.

Why'm I praying for these guys? That's obvious! They're human beings. And I remember Jesus prayed for dying crooks at his crucifixion. What else can I do right now until EMS personnel get here? I think most of the bleeding has stopped.

Then he thought of Sarah. *Where's she?* Satisfied he could do no more for the wounded, Eric searched each room in the house. No evidence of a struggle anywhere. She wasn't tied up in a closet.

Then, his cell phone rang. Sarah's name appeared on the screen! "Sarah, are you okay?"

"Of course, why wouldn't I be? I'm late getting off work. Big project to finish. I'm famished. Want to go someplace to eat?"

Eric momentarily stood speechless. Finally, he said, "Tell me where you'll be, and I'll join you in an hour." He couldn't bring himself to tell her about the mess of shattered wood and bodies scattered about her house. *How do I explain this?*

Sheriff's cars and ambulances descended on Sarah's house. Eric gave his testimony. EMTs asked if they could help Eric. "It doesn't amount to much. Go ahead and help these three guys. They need it a lot more than me."

He left exhausted. A sweaty, dirty mess, he drove home, showered, and changed clothes. His shoulder and back were both aching now. In the mirror he could barely see the shoulder wound. He tried to apply antiseptic solution but couldn't reach it. *I met my neighbors in the next apartment last month. They seem like decent people. And she's a nurse! Maybe she can help.* He walked to their door and knocked.

A middle-aged woman with short blond hair answered. "Can I help you?"

"Yes, ma'am, I hope so. I'm your neighbor. We met a month ago. I've run into a bit of a problem. I'm really embarrassed to ask, but I know you're a nurse. Could you help me apply a couple bandages?"

Alice Harmon smiled. "No problem. Come on in and have a chair. You remember my husband, Ted?"

"Hi, Ted. Sorry to bother you folks. I'm a private investigator and sometimes I get in the way of a criminal's bullet or piece of shrapnel."

"Let me see what you have here." Eric took off his shirt and she gasped. "You do have some nasty wounds. Hang on while I get some supplies." She proceeded to clean the wounds, administer antiseptic, and apply proper bandages. "Good thing you let me take care of this. You don't want these to get infected."

"Thanks so much! I just couldn't reach them myself."

"You'd better let me do this again when you need it."

"I appreciate the offer. I'll be back knocking on your door!"

"Whenever I'm home."

After dressing, Eric drove to the restaurant. *How can I tell Sarah about what happened? How do I describe a nightmare that's real?* He sighed, dreading the description she must hear. His own emotional shock left him with few words to describe her beautiful home, now splintered by bullets, spotted with blood, cordoned off with yellow tape, and crawling with deputies.

Sarah came directly from work to their favorite restaurant. She loved Italian food, and Antonio's "Best in Little Rock" status drew her and Eric again and again. Fortunately, she didn't go home to change but arrived at the restaurant early. Sarah ordered for them both since she knew what Eric would want to eat. She lounged in a comfortable chair at their favorite table while sipping delicious sweet tea.

I had a good day at the office. An important legal case is done, and my boss is finally relaxed. I enjoy my work with Stan. He's cordial and easy to work for. He makes my job as his legal secretary far from boring. And he involves me in his cases. I guess I like details and love to catch problems.

As she savored the tea, Sarah wondered what Eric might tell about his day. *I hope he's alright. He sounded stressed on the phone. And that car bomb! What's he into now? His work carries a lot of risk. I wonder how I'd be able to deal with all this excitement if we decide to marry. Would I be okay not knowing if he'll come home in one piece or not?*

Danger followed Eric like a shadow in late afternoon sunshine. *How could I kiss someone goodbye in the morning and not know if I'll see him again?* Sarah rarely dwelled on the negatives of life, but Eric's escapades kept cropping up.

The flip side of the coin excited her. Eric's work held a certain fascination. Never routine, his stories made for great conversation and table chatter.

When Eric arrived, he looked worn out. Sarah smiled and gave him an inviting kiss. "What's up?" she asked. She touched his shoulder and he winced.

"What's wrong? Are you hurt?" She noticed both tears in his jacket.

An hour later, Eric finished disgorging the contents of his day. Sarah sat spellbound. She assumed her home was safe now that Arkwell Oil crooks who drilled holes on her land either departed this world or ended up in jail. Now, invasion happened again, but this time three men waited inside to kill Eric. *What if I'd come home first?* It gave her chills to think about what such men might do.

And the man Sophia shot; what did he really want, and why was Eric in the middle of all this? She swallowed hard and looked with fear at Eric. She sat in stunned silence for some time before speaking in a shaky voice. "Eric, is all this running around, escaping exploding cars, shooting people, watching people die, being shot . . . is it worth it?"

Eric paused in his exhaustion and looked into those beautiful-but-worried hazel eyes. Sarah seemed to always ask the right questions. *How can I answer with anything that makes sense to somebody besides me? I want her to understand, but how?*

He began hesitantly, "Well, I'm a geologist and private detective. I guess there aren't many like me. I like to solve problems. That involves gathering evidence and assembling it into a model that makes sense. I get so involved I lose track of time. You know this all too well, since I'm sometimes late for our dates."

Sarah smiled and nodded that she understood. "I know you'll be late. It doesn't bother me all that much. But people trying to kill you bothers me a lot! How am I supposed to feel about your being in danger?" She began to weep.

Eric came to her side and wrapped his arms around her. He didn't know what to say.

"I love you so much, Eric," she managed, through her tears. "I don't want to lose you! Do you understand?"

He managed to sigh and say, in a halting voice, "I know. This is a terrible burden for you to carry. And it bothers me a lot. I hate using my gun to harm people. And I feel awful that you . . ." He couldn't finish his sentence.

She sniffed and reached for a tissue. Clearing her throat, she said, "How bad are your shoulder and back wounds?"

"Oh, they hurt. But folks next door are helpful. She's a nurse and bandaged me. They said to come back for a redo. That should keep me out of the ER." He tried a little humor to reduce her stress.

"I want to mend your jacket. Leave it with me." She took a deep breath and said, "Go on with your story. I want to hear you talk about why you love your work."

Eric took a breath and talked about his love for geology and solving crimes. After a pause he said, "I get to help people with their problems. That's the real driver in my career."

Sarah saw the excitement in Eric's eyes as he talked. She knew he spoke about something that came from deep within. *I love to hear him talk. I just wish he'd be safe. He shows such passion for what he does. Eric never bores me and that makes him even more attractive!*

Eric's emotional tone shifted. "And there's something extra about private detective work. I know this sounds corny, but I want to see good prevail. Call me old-fashioned, but I believe there's good and evil in the world. I want the good to win. It's part of my religious upbringing."

His face darkened and emotion filled his voice, "Now, about all this shooting people; that's a downer. I killed my first criminal defending you and me at your house during the Arkwell case. Now I've shot and wounded three more, also in your house. I hope they survive." His face grimaced. "And I pray for every person I shoot. Does that sound weird?" Sarah reached out and took his hand. He relaxed when he felt her touch. Sarah sensed his love for people. She gave him a kind face, so he knew she tuned into his feelings. "Someday I may catch a bullet. It might be fatal or not, but the possibility exists." He looked straight at Sarah and asked, "How do you feel about that?"

Sarah took all this in. She took a deep breath, let it out slowly, and then said, "I admit killing people is against my upbringing and my spiritual being. I also know we can't have criminals running rampant over the countryside, maiming and murdering innocent people. I appreciate the police and sheriff and all they do; we must have them. And private detectives, like you, are necessary to root out wrong-doing and solve crimes. It worries me that someday I might receive a phone call from the hospital, or worse, telling me you're shot. I have a hard time dealing with those thoughts hanging over my head."

Eric felt Sarah's hand tighten on his. He squeezed her hand in return and said, "Thank you." He looked into her eyes and saw that she understood. *What a woman.*

A waiter came to their table and asked if the food upset Eric. Sarah laughed, "No, the food is wonderful. We're just discussing a personal matter. Everything in your excellent restaurant is fine. We love to come here. You do great work." The waiter left scratching his head. He was glad the chef hadn't goofed and hoped this wouldn't affect his tip.

Sarah spoke quietly, "I do understand, and I support you. God is with you and that comforts me. I just need to work through how not to worry so much."

"I'll try to be careful."

Sarah released Eric's hand and picked up a fork. She continued to smile as she stabbed a piece of cold broccoli. "Good, then it's agreed. I'll try not to worry, and you'll try to stay safe! Deal?"

"Deal!"

The atmosphere around their table relaxed. Dark clouds over their heads slowly drifted away. Sarah smiled. *I'm glad I brought up the subject.*

Eric breathed a sigh of relief. *Whew! I finally got to tell her what I hadn't said before.*

For a while their conversation drifted to lighter topics.

Still in the back of Eric's mind moved the nagging question of what could be so significant about Abe McDonnell's farm that Overshoot Mining resorted to murder to retain mining rights. One hired assassin was dead. Three more were in the hospital in a bizarre effort to extinguish any opposition to what was printed in Abe's will. *Big money must be the bottom line! Nothing else makes sense, yet.*

After Eric and Sarah finished their cold dinner, the staff began to shutter the restaurant. Other customers paid their bills and left. Eric felt a tinge of guilt and left a hefty tip for the anxious waiter. Their deep discussion took longer than their mealtime.

"I can't take you home to a bullet-riddled house. The sheriff's officers have it taped off and repair will take some time." *I'd offer for her to stay at my apartment, but that'd be a bad idea! Our evening is already saturated with emotion.* "Do you mind if I call Devon and Fran and ask them if you can stay there?"

"Of course. Those wonderful people took me in during those awful days of the Arkwell case."

Devon and Fran were friends from Eric's church. He called and they were excited for Sarah to stay with them until her house was repaired.

Eric drove behind Sarah's car to their place. *I guess I'm paranoid since I remember when she was kidnapped.* After seeing her safely to Fran and Devon's door, he squeezed her hands and kissed her with a renewed affection.

"Wait!" Sarah stopped Eric and said, "Pull off that jacket and let me mend it. Fran has everything I need. This is the same one I mended earlier. I know it well."

"You got it, thanks!" He smiled as he returned to his rental car. He looked back at Sarah holding his damaged jacket, minus his Glock and the multitude of other stuff he carried in his pockets. These essentials sat on the front seat. Fortunately, Eric had backup jackets in his apartment. He stocked up when he found them at a bargain sale. To hold everything a geologist-detective needs requires a special garment.

Sleep came with difficulty. He could almost feel bullets whiz by him in Sarah's house. His wounds ached but sleep brought some relief. Again, and again he dreamed of squeezing the trigger on his Glock and hearing someone fall to the floor in her bedroom. The evening's traumas woke him during the night. Whenever he turned the wrong way, his shoulder told him to turn the other direction.

Chapter 7

Eric's phone rang and he stared at the clock as he mumbled, "Overslept again. Too much late-night action!"

It was Megan. "When're you coming in? I've got lots of data for you to digest about the Overshoot bunch."

"Be there in 45 minutes! Thanks for the wakeup call."

Eric knocked on his neighbors' door. "Sorry to bother, but I wonder if you could help with my bandages."

"Glad to do what I can." As she replaced bandages Alice said, "Your wounds certainly reflect an exciting life."

"Yeah, I usually don't get involved with clients who've got violent opponents, but recently that's changed."

"I think I saw you on a TV interview. Is that correct?"

"Guilty! Sorry you have to see me in this condition."

"Oh, no problem here! I see lots of gunshot wounds in the ER. That's my current post. Your take-down of that bogus oil company was something."

"Thanks. I'd rather do things other than chasing gangsters. Not my forte."

"Got it. Looks like you may not be out of the woods in that category yet."

Eric sighed. "You may be onto something there! Thanks for patching me up."

"I'm on the graveyard shift so you caught me when I'm home."

After first aid treatment, he gulped quickly brewed coffee and barely moist cereal. Running to his rental car, he remembered somebody tried to bomb him. After a careful search, the car appeared clean. Just to be safe, he stood well away from it and pressed the remote starter button. *No more shrapnel please.*

Sure enough, an explosion rocked the parking lot by his apartment. Pieces of the poor rental car rained down and fire erupted. He was far enough away to miss car fragments. Eric groaned. *Not another exploding car! What can I tell the rental people?* Fortunately, no other vehicles stood in the lot, and damage mainly involved his car. *These guys rigged an explosive to the ignition system so I couldn't easily locate it.* He speed-dialed police and fire departments.

Alice ran out of their building. "Are you alright?"

"Yep. Just a bit surprised. They hid the explosive well."

"Whew! What a mess!"

"Got that right. My day is starting with a bang."

She laughed guardedly. "You seem to take this rather light-heartedly. Are you sure you aren't experiencing any head trauma?"

"Ask me any questions before the EMTs get here. I think I can answer who the president is, and I know the day of the week."

"Guess you have things under control. See you tomorrow for rebandaging. And try not to take any more bullets or shrapnel."

He waved her off with a smile. Sirens wailed as officers and fire fighters converged on Eric's parking lot. Eric made his statement; then he called the rental company. "My job seems to involve risk to your cars. I've lost another one." He hailed a cab to take him to his office. Somehow, he couldn't bring himself to ask for another rental just then.

How does this failed attempt on my life affect the company's attitude toward their hired killers? Will Overshoot Mining give this new person a second chance to kill me? One deceased hired gun filled a slot in the morgue. Others were in the hospital. *The supply of criminals hasn't dried up yet. Will it? As the job gets more difficult to pull off, do the rewards increase? What are they paying these people? What's my value as a corpse?* Then he thought of Sarah. *Better let her know; otherwise she'll hear about it on the news.* Reluctantly he punched her number on his phone.

Eric cringed at Sarah's reaction, "Eric! Not again! Are you hurt? What're you going to do?"

"I'm not injured. Just a bit shaken. And, I can't give up on the case. In some ways, I've just begun. I'm on my way to the office in a cab. Maybe I'll use these for a while until things quiet down."

The other end of the phone conversation was silent for a long moment. Then Sarah spoke with quavering voice, "Eric, do you need protection?"

Her question shook Eric. He protected other people. He couldn't imagine needing protection. Such a thought never occurred to him. *Ridiculous! Anyway, who'd I ask to protect me?* After some reflection he cleared his voice and answered, "I appreciate the thought, Sarah. But I'll be very careful."

This didn't satisfy Sarah, but she was impatiently learning when to push and when to draw back. If the conversation went much further, it wouldn't help their relationship. "Okay, but I'll feel better if I know what you do to keep safe."

So, Eric leaned back in the taxi seat and told Sarah how he approached vehicles before he started the engine or opened a door, about how he changed routes that he routinely traveled, and how, when being tailed, he could avoid contact with bad guys.

Sarah listened to Eric's list and shifted in her chair. She sighed and appeared only mildly appeased. They agreed to let the topic alone for the time being. They rang off, with promises to pray for each other.

The taxi driver spoke over his shoulder, "Ya must have a great woman. She sure does care about ya!"

"You got that right." He paid the driver and walked through his office door.

Megan confronted him with hands on her hips. "Eric Bonfield; what are you doing, barely escaping bullets and exploding cars?"

Caught off-guard, Eric's shoulders slumped, and he stared at the floor. "Megan, you ask the most impossible questions! I guess I'm a magnet for somebody's hunks of metal and explosives."

"That doesn't answer my question. I love my job here and I want to continue working for you, but that won't happen if you end up on the wrong side of somebody's ire."

"I know, I know. Why I get these kinds of cases is beyond me. All I know is that it's my work. Somebody's got to do it. I guess it's me."

She smiled, removed her hands from her hips, and hugged Eric. "And I think you're the best guy for the job!" Eric cringed when she touched his shoulder and back. Megan flushed pink and asked, "Does that hurt?"

"Just a couple flesh wounds from a bullet and a flying fragment of a car."

"Should you see a doctor?"

"No, there's a nurse next door who's keeping me together."

Megan shook her head. "You amaze me sometimes . . . maybe all the time." Then she turned to sit down at her computer. Without another word, she started to send e-mails to clients.

Eric stood a bit dumbfounded. He never knew what to expect from his office manager. Then he looked at his desk and whistled his amazement. The array of documents Megan found on the strange company named Overshoot Mining, Inc. stared back at him. Finding his tongue, he said, "Looks like you really found a truckload of info! Thanks, Megan."

She mumbled something and continued to type.

He sat down and began to digest the mass of data.

Joseph watched the interchange between Megan and Eric. He came over and crossed his arms. "My friend," he addressed Eric this way when he wanted to make a point, "you seem to be the target of someone who doesn't like you very much."

"Now that is the understatement of the morning," Eric said. "I've got a sign on my back that says, 'shoot me' or 'blow me up'".

Joseph smiled and said, "It makes me think my work is dull. I finally found the missing boy and returned him to his family. They were very happy."

"Great. Good work. Now, how about helping me wade through this pile of stuff that Megan found on my not-so-friendly mining company nemesis?"

"Sure. I can help."

"Excellent. Start with this pile." He divided the stack between them.

It took all morning for Eric and Joseph to read state records and online references to Overshoot Mining. They took notes, talked as they read, and argued about everything. Finally, Eric said, "This company is successful at creating a maze of dead ends and roadblocks. Their company law folk must major in obscurity. It's impossible to learn what's going on in their mines."

They broke for lunch with Eric riding in Joseph's car to a local pizza hole-in-the-wall. Dining on slices of greasy carbohydrates, they summarized Megan's findings. Wiping his hands on a brown paper napkin, Joseph said, "Eric, I get the feeling this company purposely tries to confuse anyone who wants to investigate them."

Swallowing a bite of pepperoni, Eric replied, "I think they've figured out how to answer just enough on the state forms, so they commit themselves to very little. They avoid all appearance of doing anything."

Joseph asked, "How can a company survive without actually showing a profit for the mines they operate?"

"Got me. This smells of something criminal, but they're very clever at hiding any evidence. The company documents are useless for our purposes. The only thing I found slightly helpful was the disclosure of salaries. Everyone is paid well, but not so well that red flags wave. Even the CEO doesn't make an immoral salary. I wonder if there're any offshore accounts. I don't have experience finding this sort of information. I understand it can be done, but I've never done it."

Joseph smiled. "Eric, I have some distant relatives in Mexico who used to be part of a money laundering operation. They served time in jail and are now out and seem to be rehabilitated. I wonder if they could check out the foreign account actions of Overshoot Mining."

"Joseph, your connections amaze me! Go for it!"

After they returned from lunch, Joseph contacted his relatives. Speaking in rapid-fire Spanish, Joseph enthusiastically worked the phone for an hour.

Eric checked his notes to see if he missed any connections that he should follow up on. Josephine and Sophia were safely watched. The precious diary and old will were locked securely away. *I've got to contact Sean McDonnell and bring him up to date.* He left Joseph in animated phone conversation about something, but Eric could not make heads nor tails of it.

Facing the music and requesting another rental car, Eric sheepishly accepted keys from a smiling agent. "You do keep us busy, Mr. Bonfield. I'm glad we only have to replace the cars."

"You and me both! And thanks for the remote starter. You don't rent pickups, do you?"

"Only for non-explosive clients!" She laughed quietly.

"Touché!"

He carefully drove to McDonnell's office while keeping a lookout for any vehicles following too close to be normal.

By now, McDonnell's secretary knew to usher Eric directly into her boss's office without asking. McDonnell and Eric spent an hour going over the events since they last talked. Sean shook his head again and again during Eric's litany.

After Eric paused from exhaustion, McDonnell said, "I'll have my attorneys go over the old will, the diary, and the newest will, plus take sworn testimony from Josephine and Sophia. We'll do what's necessary to see that Sophia validates this last-minute will. I don't know if there's enough to nullify the bogus will and contract. I don't trust their company lawyers any farther than I can kick them. Overshoot will bring in big gun attorneys to try and destroy the ladies' testimonies. I think we'll need more than this diary and their testimonies to turn the tide."

"You may be right. I'm no lawyer," Eric said, "but my partner is looking to see if there might be some money laundering going on. He has connections who may help in discovery."

"Good! As a businessperson, I can't see how those people can continue operating mines with virtually no profit. They're either very inept or are very clever!"

"I tend to think the latter. I hope the three wounded assassins can be pumped for information, but they first need to be well enough to talk. Another concern is your safety and mine. So far, shots and explosions have come my way. But you're a visible person around Little Rock. Someone with a high-powered rifle might try to get a shot at you!"

"Why they haven't targeted me is a puzzle," said McDonnell.

Eric's phone buzzed and his screen read "Police." "Just a minute, Mr. McDonnell, this might be important."

He listened to the message and sat up in his chair with a look of horror on his face. "Mr. McDonnell, a man entered the hospital, overpowered the guard to Josephine's room, and attempted to kill her in the hospital bed!"

Sean McDonnell sat speechless. They stared at each other, dumbfounded at this brazen act in broad daylight. McDonnell finally managed to ask, "Is she alright? Did they catch him?"

"No, they didn't find the guy. His escape was well planned. Hospital security didn't catch wind of the break-in until it was too late. Video cameras captured his actions and police put out an APB. The guard was rendered unconscious by injection, and Josephine received a near lethal dose of some chemical. Apparently, she's in a coma. I'd better get down there to see what I can discover." He left Sean McDonnell slumped in his chair, staring into space. His usual gruffness was gone.

On the way to the hospital, Eric rubbed his temples. He couldn't comprehend the audacity of these people. His mind returned to McDonnell's question, "What're they trying to hide?"

The whole thing strained Eric's rational mind and almost made him sick. He'd dealt with murderers before, but this current bunch made anyone else seem like kindergarten pranksters. *These people are ruthless, cold-blooded killers.* He thought of Sarah's concern for his safety. *Will this group succeed in cutting my life short?*

Temptation crept into Eric's mind to drop the whole case and go back to the safety of solving sinkhole problems. Shaking his head to clear out such thoughts, he knew he couldn't imagine giving up the case if these people roamed freely. *God must've put me here to do something about this. I can't quit now.*

At the hospital, Eric identified himself. The guard awakened by the time Eric arrived. He attempted to answer questions from other officers. Eric listened in and asked, "Did anyone visit Josephine from the time she came to the hospital until now?"

The guard showed Eric the visitors log. Eric scanned it and made a note to talk with each person to see if she gave any evidential statements. He asked to see Josephine's room and began a thorough search. After looking through what little personal material remained, Eric found three sheets of paper stuffed inside a Gideon Bible. The notes outlined the same things Sophia had said about the company lawyer, Overshoots representatives, and Abe's illness. Josephine had signed the note and dated it. Amazingly, a notary public's stamp embossed the sheets. Eric heaved a sigh of relief. *One of Josephine's visitors was a notary! I hope she makes it, but if not, she's given us some key eyewitness evidence.*

Eric asked the officer in charge of the investigation to consider the papers as evidence related to the attempted murder. She bagged the sheets and sent it to evidence storage at the police station.

How can I crack Overshoot Mining's code of silence? All the verbosity he read in the company's reports to the state amounted to nothing but gibberish. Maybe they fulfilled the letter of the law, but Eric could not find a clue about what they might be doing on Abe's McDonnell's farm. After pushing around some soil and rock, nothing seemed to come of it. And their justification, what little there was, made no sense.

He slept little that night. Early the next morning, he was jarred awake by a sudden thought. *Hospital video captured the killer's image, and he could easily be identified.* If this thug was captured, he might finger someone in the company and spill the identity of his employer.

Eric dressed and hurriedly left for his office after grabbing a quick breakfast. The car rental company now classified Eric as a high-risk person, so he was restricted to "junkers." They grew tired of losing newer models. He pushed the remote starter, just to be safe. The car coughed into activity without blowing apart. *Nice!*

As Eric drove, his senses told him someone was following in a dark car. The car always stayed within a block of his. *I wonder if I should try to ditch the tail or trap the occupant and get some answers.* Eric's curiosity refused to do a simple ditch job, so he called a contact at the police department and suggested a plan to catch the tail. Patrol cars would take up positions to trap whoever might be following Eric. He maneuvered onto side streets as he pretended to dodge the follower. Then he backed into an alley and waited.

His breathing drew short as Eric strained to see if the tail would take the bait. No car appeared. Whoever followed should've passed by now. Then he looked in his rear-view mirror. A second car slowly came up behind him. *Wow. These guys are good.* Eric lurched his car out of the alley and onto the street, just in time to see the first car approaching not 50 feet away. He jammed the accelerator, screeched his tires, and careened away from his pursuers. *Whew! That was too close!*

The car in the alley tried to negotiate a turn onto the street just as the first car accelerated. Eric heard the crash of metal on metal as the two cars collided. *What a break!* Eric called his location to police, and they descended on the scene. Wailing sirens were coming from two directions. *I hoped for a more silent approach, but it's too late to complain.*

The pursuers were trapped since their cars sat immobilized. Eric saw them bolt from their damaged vehicles and run in opposite directions. Two fugitives emerged; one from each car. Eric contacted police and described how to block the criminals' escape. He calculated where they might run, so he drove to cut off one of them.

Careening around the block, Eric saw a man running down an alley and accelerated after him. The man saw Eric coming fast and tried to dodge out of the way, but the alley dead ended. The man drew a gun. Eric ducked as the bullet smashed into his windshield.

Eric tried to apply the brakes but being hunched over did not work well for hitting the pedal. As he struggled to stop, a dull thud and jolt shook Eric's car as it struck a building wall. The air bag exploded. Pushing the bag away, Eric jumped from the car and saw, to his dismay, the man racing up the alley. *Another link to Overshoot Mining gone.*

Police unsuccessfully chased the second driver. After Eric gave the officers his report, he called the rental car company with the news about another wrecked car. Happy campers, they? Not so much. Fortunately, Eric bought excellent insurance. That reduced the company's frustration a little. Eric called Megan and explained his situation. He needed another car and had to wait for delivery.

Megan took a deep breath, exhaled, and said, "Eric, how do you get into these scrapes?"

"I wish I knew!"

He called Sarah and told her about his latest escapade.

She exuded no happiness but thanked God for his safety. "When will I see you again?"

"I don't know. I've got to get to the office and sort things out. Can we meet tonight after your work? My days are so unpredictable."

Sarah sighed and said, "Yes, and please don't tell me another story about how you just missed being killed!"

"I'll do my best. I love you."

Sarah's rigidity melted a little. She breathed into the phone, "And I love you."

After a half-hour passed, another dilapidated car found its way to Eric with the obligatory remote starter. *I hope the wrecked car is repairable.* He thanked the rental driver and drove more casually to his office. *No need to hurry. Those missing criminals need to find other cars too!* On the way Eric realized he might have dropped his guard too easily. *What's the price on my head? It must be high.* He gunned the engine, which sputtered due to its high mileage, and his vehicle limped to Eric's office.

The office was Eric's sanctuary. Megan kept everything organized. Even with stacks of things to do, order prevailed. All materials found their position by priority. Megan learned what Eric considered important and kept those on top of his pile. His computer screen was arranged in order of importance too. *What an office manager! She'd better not leave or I'm done!*

Joseph sat calmly going through his stack as he sorted out what he thought Eric would prefer to deal with. Joseph's mind processed information much like Eric's. Rarely did they get upset with each other. But they had spirited disagreements.

After another brief phone conversation in Spanish, Joseph looked up and said, "My contacts in Mexico are working on possible offshore accounts belonging to Overshoot Mining, but it may take some time to find any. These guys are either very sophisticated or don't bother with offshore."

"I don't see how anyone can find this stuff."

Joseph smiled ruefully and said, "Having been on the wrong side of the law, they know how such things work."

Eric turned to his desk. With a hint of guilt, he wondered if he was neglecting the consulting side of his business. His eyes fell on a note from a client in a rural area near Abe's farm. The man complained about a well pumping out awful tasting water. *Gotta check this out!* "Joseph. Could you take some samples from this farmer's well and have them analyzed? Something odd's going on and it might be related to this mining case."

"Will do."

Joseph knew protocol for water collection and assumed that role in the firm. If not done correctly, accidental contamination by the person collecting samples might easily ruin evidence. Joseph quickly learned how to avoid this problem. After gathering supplies, he started to leave the office. "Megan, I may not be back until tomorrow. By the time I grab samples and take them to the analytical lab it may be after dark."

"Got it. I'll keep Eric's nose to the grindstone while you're gone." She grinned in Eric's direction. He was so engrossed at the contents on his computer screen that he hardly knew what she said.

The office phone rang. Megan said, "Eric, wake up! It's the police." He shook himself and answered. To his dismay, although officers scoured the neighborhood, they still couldn't come up with any leads on either driver. *Where'd Overshoot Mining find these people? They're good at what they do and hard to catch.*

Eric thanked the officer and the phone hung limp in his hand. *What a waste of human life to always be outside the law.* Eric paused and prayed for people affected by all the mayhem.

What's so important on Abe's farm that they hire all these gunmen? Eric felt depressed. Finally, he shifted back to his work stack. "I've got to keep the geological consulting side on par with investigating crimes. Otherwise, I lose perspective on what's important," he mumbled.

Megan heard Eric muttering. She said nothing. It was clear the case ate at his mind. Lunch time came and went. He felt no hunger. *Got to keep up with all this work.* By mid-afternoon Eric made it through his stack. He dictated responses and reports and finally sat back in his chair to take a deep breath. The chair creaked. He was about to ask Megan to order a new chair when the phone rang. Megan called out, "It's Sean McDonnell."

"Eric! I heard about your scrape with those guys. Are you injured?"

"I'm fine. But I'm frustrated so many people are after me, or us. Have you experienced any strange sightings?"

McDonnell said, "Nobody is after me just yet. But I've come up with another of Abe's relatives who you might check on. Her name is Frances McDonnell. She wasn't close to Josephine or Sophia, but I think Abe had her in his circle of confidants. She's a niece and, for some reason, he trusted her with information the others may not have been privy to."

Eric quickly wrote down the name, address, and phone number. "I'll pay her a visit." After he hung up, Eric excitedly called Frances McDonnell and arranged to meet with her. Then he told Megan where he was going. "Don't expect me back today."

"Eric, you know I never expect to see you except when I see you!" She laughed.

"You know me too well."

"Just so you know, today is Saturday and I don't usually work weekends. But I knew how busy you've been with this mining case, so I came in. This is a reminder that tomorrow is Sunday and I won't be here. Going to church?"

Eric slapped his head! "Of course! I so easily lose track of days. Thanks for the reminder. I'll see you there."

The car rental agency's sedan was worse than the wrecks he sent to the junk yard. Staring at the heap of plastic and metal, Eric shook his head and grumbled, "I wish I had my pickup." His beloved F-150 still resided in evidence lockdown waiting to be released for repairs. "I know I'm hard on vehicles," Eric said to the excuse-for-a-car. "Or is it that others are hard on my cars? I think George Washington last rented you." The rental company was onto him.

Chapter 8

Fortunately, the latest rental car started and sputtered down the road to Eric's appointment. Frances McDonnell lived in a rural area off the main highways like most of the family members he met. The exception was Sean. Sean's home sat in a moderately well-off subdivision of Little Rock. Sean didn't flaunt his money and his home showed it. It was ample, but not what one would expect for such a successful businessman. So far, the villains of Overshoot Mining avoided targeting his residence. *That might be too obvious and hurt their case in court.*

Frances McDonnell's home looked like it could use a coat of paint. A set of Arkansas hounds greeted Eric with a few mournful attempts at pretending to be guard dogs. A middle-aged woman's head with medium length brown hair appeared at the door and silenced the dogs with a sharp reprimand. She wore no glasses but had a sparkle in her eyes that betrayed sharp wit and clear understanding. Eric suspected he was in for an interesting interview.

Eric showed her his credentials and reminded her of his call. The interior of Frances' home did not match those of other family members he'd met. Her living room was smartly appointed and exuded refinement. For some reason the inside didn't match the exterior. Eric would later learn she graduated from Vanderbilt with high honors. He never learned why she chose to return to her Highlands homeland.

None of the McDonnell women would be considered ravishing beauties. Sarah had nothing to worry about. Eric soon learned that all the McDonnell kinfolk he would encounter held high moral standards and possessed fierce independence. *I like these people. They're real and without pretenses. I feel more at home with rural Highlands folk than with some townies who're concerned with appearances and what others think about them. I like real people with real problems. It's easier to work with them.* He didn't have to peek around masks that covered shallow lives.

Eric asked about Frances' relationship to Abe McDonnell and what she knew about the will, the contract, and his death. For the next three hours he wrote furiously in his notebook. She possessed an amazing memory and could recount days, times, and details with pinpoint accuracy. The story closely matched Josephine's diary, but with more details and shocks. Frances was indeed Abe's confidant. Abe talked with others, but Frances knew the real ins and outs of his life. Frances listened well; plus, she took lots of notes, dated them, and even had them notarized! Eric was wide-eyed. *This woman is a gold mine of information. She speaks without much of her heritage dialect. Must have adapted to living someplace else before moving back here.* The story of Abe began to unfold in detail.

Abe and his wife lived on an 80-acre farm. As far as Frances knew, they were reasonably happy but had no children. Abe was the local go-to fixit guy. Farmers and suburban dwellers alike knew Abe as the one to contact whenever any type of mechanical equipment needed patching up. His large barn contained a multitude of tools, equipment, and parts. On rainy days, large farm machinery could be pulled inside the barn. This allowed him to work in comfort. People sought Abe to fix everything from broken hand tools to tractor engines to hay bailers. He was an expert welder and very creative. Many people would come to him with their ideas and he would transform pieces of metal into useable products. Friends told Abe that he ought to patent his creations. He never bothered. "Too busy havin' fun," was his excuse.

To augment his income as a fixit person, Abe raised Hereford cattle. He was proud of the fine stock he maintained. It wasn't a large herd, because his farm only had so much grassland.

Life was good for Abe. Then he lost his wife. He was depressed for a time but managed to move on with life by spending more time doing repairs for people and building up the quality of his livestock. Somewhat gregarious, Abe loved to have kinfolk come to visit, so he could talk about what interested him. However, Abe's financial and business matters were strictly forbidden topics. Few knew anything about his income or other personal dealings. His health was also not discussed. Abe fit the model of an independent highlander.

But then came a geologist knocking on his door and suggesting he was sitting on a valuable deposit of ore. Overshoot Mining personnel started pressuring him to have them open a mine. Abe didn't like these "city slickers" and resisted their stories of grandeur and wealth. He listened to their promises but didn't buy most of their stories.

Eric hadn't known the details about where meetings with the Overshoot gang were held. They always wanted to take Abe out for lunch or dinner or breakfast. It didn't matter which meal he chose, but they insisted on a specific restaurant where they could talk. The real reason was to be away from prying ears of nosey relatives. Abe enjoyed food and took them up on their offers. Eric's eyes opened wider when he learned the restaurant matched his first meeting place with Sean — the one with the exploding Jaguar!

Why had Sean used the same restaurant as Abe? Frances provided an answer. Many of the McDonnell clan liked the simple but abundant fare the restaurant provided. Being inexpensive helped too. None of the McDonnells liked to spend money.

Overshoot Mining reps bought Abe whatever food he liked, and the same waiter served them. In fact, the owner of the restaurant seemed to hover nearby throughout the meal, asking about food quality and fussing around their table. Josephine and Sophia's stories lacked such detail. Frances was an expert at remembering information. Abe was selective with whom he shared his business ventures and she was definitely a major player in his inner circle. In fact, Frances was his most in-depth confidant.

Eric's mind filled with questions. *Why'd the Overshoot group choose this restaurant? Why the same waiter? Why'd the owner pay them so much attention?* Then, as Frances talked, Eric wondered about the exploding Jaguar. *Why blow up the owner's car? Not a case of mistaken identity. They knew it was his, not Sean's. What about the owner's integrity? Where'd the proprietor of a small country café get the cash to buy a Jag? Was it a payment under the counter for something special?* Eric knew he must pay the owner a visit and ask questions.

Frances continued to bubble information. She described Abe's health. No sooner had the restaurant meals started than Abe began to weaken. Normally a specimen of health, he showed rapid signs of aging. His speech became slurred, and he didn't seem to process information like he used to. His thinking became less coherent.

Josephine and Sophia worried about him and recommended that he see a doctor. Abe, ever the independent Arkansas Highland farmer, refused. But when Frances pushed him, he relented. She told him he might do something foolish if his health went further downhill. Abe finally gave in and staggered into the office of a local general practitioner. "The clinic did a blood test and found some funny stuff in his blood."

"Like what?"

Frances wasn't certain about the results. Before Abe could contact the doctor to see what the "funny stuff" might be, the physician ended up dead, shot on a country road.

Eric's eyes almost bulged. *These jokers must have poisoned Abe by spiking his food or drinks. And to kill a physician . . . what an atrocity!* "Did any of the family follow up on the medical report?"

"No." Frances said this with a grimace. "We were too concerned with his immediate health situation."

"Can you tell me the doctor's name or clinic?"

Frances remembered the name after looking in her notarized notes. Eric nodded his head and marveled at her thoroughness. He took down the clinic's information.

"Please go on," he said. "You're helping me with the investigation by all you're saying."

Frances told of Abe's continued decline in health. He seemed more and more confused. When the clowns from Outshoot showed up at Abe's house with the contract, he signed it almost unwillingly. Frances doubted Abe's ability to even know what he was signing.

About the revised will, Frances was also certain that Abe had no idea what he was signing.

"Did any family member try to intervene?"

Frances thought Josephine might have tried, but with Abe so confused she must have given up. "Catching Abe without the mining people around was difficult. They guarded their time with Abe like hawks."

"Anyone else might know about the contract signing?"

She referred to her notes. "Yes, a nephew tried to intervene. He didn't survive . . . seems he fell off a cliff while hiking in a state park."

Eric made a note to check out this "accidental" death. While Frances paused during her litany for a drink of water, he called Megan and asked for background information on the death of nephew Paul McDonnell.

Frances told of the day Abe finally signed the revised will. Abe could barely hold a pen. The Overshoot henchmen practically signed the will for him. Frances hid in the next room, peeking through a crack in the wall.

"Did anyone else see this?"

"Yes, my brother Eddy was looking through a keyhole."

"I hate to ask, but is Eddy still alive?"

"Yes."

Amazing. Eric smiled sarcastically. Frances said she and Eddy made a pact to keep quiet about what they saw until it became necessary to let it be known. Fortunately, the Overshoot people weren't aware of the eavesdroppers.

Eric shuddered when he thought he might have been followed to Frances' home. He couldn't afford to put her life in jeopardy. *I want her in a witness protection program. What should I do?* Eric got up and looked out the front window. Nothing in sight. Then he saw it. A car slowly approached the house.

Eric warned Frances to go to a secure room away from the front windows. He feared things could get dicey. The car came closer. Eric tensed as he removed the Glock from his jacket. Out of habit, he checked the magazine. The car stopped in front of Frances' house and a man stepped out. He drew a handgun from a shoulder holster. *Another hired gun!*

Perspiration broke out on Eric's forehead. Again, he faced a decision he despised. The Glock in his hand was all that separated Frances and himself from certain death. The man walked to the front door as he glanced nervously from side to side. He knocked. Eric moved to the side of the door. "Who is it?"

The man opened fire, puncturing the door with bullets. Then the man rushed the door with his shoulder and broke it down.

Here we go again! The man burst into the room but was met with bullets from Eric's gun. The intruder fell before he could discharge his weapon again. Eric surveyed the mass of legs, arms and splintered wood. He quickly checked for signs of life. The man was breathing. *Thank God!* Eric called the Hot Spring County sheriff's office and EMS. *How many times do I have to do this?*

Eric's mind whirled with questions. *This guy must have tailed me, but did he alert the Overshoot gang about Frances's address?* Eric couldn't take any chances with her life.

When a sheriff deputy arrived, Eric asked for a quick check of the intruder's car. Frances timidly came out of hiding. She stood in shock at the scene. "Do you know this man?" Eric asked.

"No! I've never seen him before." She cringed as she said this.

As EMTs were loading the intruder into an ambulance, another deputy arrived and identified the gunman as the assassin who attempted to murder Josephine in her bed. "I saw his mug in a grainy hospital camera shot." *And he looks like the person I almost ran down in the alley. This guy gets around!*

Eric asked a deputy to check the man's cell phone records. Frances was visibly shaken. Eric tried to calm her and promised she would be protected. The deputy reported the most recent phone texts indicated he was told to tail Eric. No other texts were sent or received.

The gunman was probably going to report back after finishing us off. Then he'd be paid. Whew! Perhaps Frances is safe. But what about the sheriff's radio and report? The wrong people might be listening in. Eric was assured the whole incident would be kept quiet as to location and intended victims.

Still, Eric wanted better security for his witness. He thought about hiding her. *But where?* Some of his church friends might do it. Then again, maybe she should stay at home. *I'd feel better with surveillance of Frances' place.*

Cell phone records revealed the plans laid out for Eric's demise. He chilled as he read the details. *These people are vicious.* The records glaringly omitted what might happen to the gunman if the assassination attempt failed.

This might be the killer's last chance to do the job. Failure could mean certain death for the criminal. Too many failures. Overshoot Mining fostered a hotbed for murder. Phone records indicated the thug's employer used a phone purchased from a drug store. Paying with cash avoided any trace of who purchased the phone. Such devices ended in the local landfill. No recycling for Overshoot's adjunct employees!

Eric tried to tabulate the body count of hired gunmen. They occupied either the morgue or hospital beds. *I wonder if word reaches this clientele of assassins that Overshoot Mining might be a dangerous group to work for.* From database searches, the sheriff told Eric all these people were shipped in from distant states. *Then there's Abe, Josephine, Sophia, and Frances. So many lives disrupted or ended unnecessarily.*

Exhaustion seeped into Eric's bones. He asked Frances to contact her brother and alert him that he might need to be a witness if things progressed to the courtroom stage. She agreed but wanted to stay at her home. Eric suggested her notarized notes be held in the sheriff's security lockup. That was fine with her. Her house would be under surveillance. After repairs were arranged for the front door, Eric felt he could leave Frances.

Wearily, Eric called Sarah and they agreed on a very late dinner. With their favorite restaurant closed for the night, they chose an all-night diner that stayed open except on Christmas and New Year's. Hardly a place for a romantic rendezvous, but Eric was in no mood for that anyway. Due to the lateness of the hour, he didn't want Sarah to drive, especially with so many dangerous persons about. So, he picked her up at Devon and Fran's house.

He dragged his body out of the vehicle and shuffled toward the front door. Sarah opened the door and took his breath away. She wore a bright yellow top and black jeans. Her hair was down and curled to frame her face. His weariness seemed to instantly evaporate.

He sighed and said, "Hi Beautiful, you look fantastic."

She gave him a radiant smile and grasped his hands in hers. "My heroic crime fighter, survivor in the battle of evil versus good, and the only person I want to be with."

Eric sighed. He took her hand and said with a flourish, "Ma'am, may I escort you to my rented chariot?"

"Why, yes, sir. Thank you."

He walked her to the dilapidated car. It could've passed for a 19th century stagecoach ready for the trash heap, but Sarah didn't mind. *Eric can take me for a ride on a hay wagon for all I care. I'm with him and nothing else matters.* She sat as close to him as her well-worn seat belt would allow. Sarah stroked his arm and nuzzled his neck with her nose.

"Sarah, please stop; I'm driving." His voice was anything but sincere, so she paid no attention to his request.

The late-night diner provided minimum ambiance. Sarah's day held no emotional candle to the traumatic events Eric experienced. He tried hard to maintain interest in her side of the conversation. When his turn came, he told of the shootout with a hired assassin.

As she studied his facial expressions, Sarah wondered what it would be like to be married to Eric. *How would I hold up waiting for him to return from some dangerous investigation?* She shook the idea from her mind when she realized she missed part of his passionate retelling of the day.

"Sorry. Would you mind repeating the last part?"

Eric blinked. *Normally Sarah listens intently.* He shrugged and backtracked his story. A thought drifted through his mind. *It'd be wonderful to always have her near me to hear my stories of failure and success. How great would that be? And she's so easy on the eyes.*

Eventually the diner held only two customers: Sarah and Eric. He was out of steam and Sarah's eyes began to droop. Eric paid the bill and drove Sarah to her temporary residence. As they approached Devon and Fran's front porch, he said, "I wonder if the day will come when we'll walk through a front door, and I won't leave?"

"I hope so," she responded with a grin.

"Megan thinks it's a good idea to see someone about premarital counseling. It really helped their decision to get married. Could you check into this for us?"

"Let me see what I can manage," she said brightening.

"Go for it. By the way, church tomorrow?"

"Pick me up?"

"Wouldn't miss the opportunity. Do you mind going to the late morning service? I'm exhausted and need some sleep."

"As long as it's with you, I've no preference." Sarah made eyes at him.

On the trip home Eric thought about the case that consumed most of his waking moments. *I've got to check out the restaurant owner. Why was his Jag blown up? Did he know about Abe being drugged? I'll hit him Monday.*

Eric made it to his apartment without falling asleep at the wheel. He collapsed in bed.

Chapter 9

Sunday morning came as usual, but Eric slept in. He wandered out of bed in time to ask Alice for a rebandage of his wounds before he picked up Sarah. After lunch, they spent the afternoon leisurely reading at the public library. He was glad for a day to recuperate from a frenzied week and let his body heal from wounds provided courtesy of Overshoot Mining. Eric's eyes closed a few times as he forced himself to enjoy a novel. It wasn't a detective story! They shared a light supper but skipped watching a movie. Both were too tired.

On Monday, Eric awoke refreshed. He decided to take his time getting this week off the ground. Instead of an instant breakfast, he ate a balanced meal in his apartment. *Why begin today in frustration? No point.*

Alice provided fresh bandages. "You're lucky I'm on a late shift at ER. And you're healing nicely. No infection. Now try to avoid any further bullets!" She smiled.

"My idea exactly! Thanks so much for your skill."

Walking onto the parking lot, he checked his car. The remote starter worked but nothing unusual happened to the car. No bombs found their way to destroy the rental car overnight. *What a great way to start the day!*

Things looked even better when Megan greeted him with a short stack of work. A message from the Hot Spring County sheriff's office assured him the man he shot would live, and his profile matched someone wanted by Indiana authorities on murder charges. Criminals in the hospitals were talking to interrogators, but none of the killers knew who hired them. Everything was done anonymously by phone and payment handled via mailbox drops.

An email message from the officer who ran the Pulaski County jail was cryptic: "If all those guys in the hospital end up in my jail, I'll be running out of space for your 'clients', or whatever you call these people." Eric sent an email response. "I'll try to keep the crowd to a minimum." This drew a smiley emoji in return.

Eric enjoyed a good working relationship with folks employed by the police and various sheriffs' departments. He kept them busy with his cases but wished he could resolve the investigations sooner and with less violence. The Overshoot case was spread mainly between Pulaski County, where Little Rock was located, and Hot Spring County, where Magnet Cove resided. He continually traveled through Saline County, since it bridged the gap between Pulaski and Hot Spring. Magnet Cove used to be a town but is now a census-designated place with very low population. Its proximity to the borders of Garland and Saline Counties meant travel through back roads of those areas was often necessary.

When I first started in this business, I was confused whenever I worked near Hot Springs, the city, since it's located in Garland County and not Hot Spring County. I remember accidently contacting the Hot Spring County sheriff in Malvern instead of the Garland County sheriff in Hot Springs! The sheriffs are good natured people and just laughed when I mistook who had jurisdiction. The Garland sheriff gave me a lengthy lesson on county history in Arkansas.

After he wrote a few reports and generated correspondence, Eric drove to the restaurant where it all started. He planned his arrival between the breakfast and lunch crowds when, he hoped, the place might be deserted. Although bumpy and riddled with potholes, the road leading to the restaurant was picturesque. Rock outcrops were a welcome diversion from grassy roadsides. *Geologists love outcrops!*

The restaurant looked unoccupied by customers when Eric arrived. Construction workers had almost completed restoration after the bombing. New windows admitted bright morning light. He asked at the cashier's station for the owner. A waiter's thumb pointed to an office behind the kitchen. Eric knocked on the door marked "Hugh Fogel, Owner", and entered. A brusque man sat at an unkempt desk as he chewed on a soggy cigar. The absence of a tobacco tray suggested Mr. Fogel didn't smoke but munched the cigar as a pacifier. Fogel was of medium height with a receding hairline. A bit of gray hair sprouted around his ears. Dark eyes pierced Eric. *That look is designed to intimidate lesser souls.*

"Help ya?"

"I'm Eric Bonfield, a private investigator. The explosion that destroyed your Jaguar has me curious. I was eating in your restaurant at the time." Eric had checked the registration and knew a few details about the car.

"Yeah, it's a real mess." Fogel shifted in his chair, obviously not comfortable discussing the subject.

"Any clues why your car was bombed?"

Fogel moved his frame before answering. "I don't know. The sheriff thought it was a case of mistaken identity."

Eric detected the man's discomfort and pressed the point. "I've a suspicion this wasn't mistaken identity, but intentional."

The man's face turned pale. His cigar nearly fell out of his mouth as he opened it to speak, but no words came out. Eric squeezed harder.

"And I suspect it had to do with one of your regular customers, or should I say several customers who brought Abe McDonnell here to dine."

The owner teetered off balance in his chair and stammered something incoherent.

"Were you involved in poisoning Mr. McDonnell's food, or spiking his drink with a toxic chemical?"

"How . . . I . . . you . . ."

With Fogel totally flustered, Eric went for the jugular, "And wasn't the bomb a way of telling you to keep your mouth shut about poisoning Abe McDonnell?"

Fogel nearly fell out of his chair. "How . . . did . . . you . . . know?"

Got the confession I want. "Some things are more obvious than others. Now I'd like you to make a statement that what you just agreed to is true. You can give this testimony to the sheriff's deputy coming in the door as we speak."

Before arriving at the restaurant, Eric suggested to the Hot Spring County sheriff that the bombing incident might be solved today and requested an officer to take a confession. The deputy walked into Fogel's office with paper and pen in hand. Before the owner could reconsider his options, and after he heard the traditional warning about an attorney, he confessed to providing the place for poisoning.

As he scribbled on the page, Fogel emphasized that he didn't realize the stuff fed to Abe might prove fatal. "I got no clue 'bout that. Thought it was sumthin' to make him do what they wanted. I just provide food."

Not until the bomb blew his car to oblivion did Fogel understand how serious the people doing business in his establishment might be. It became clear when a phone call told him that, if he didn't keep quiet, the next bomb would go off with him inside the car. Fogel was shaken and worried about what might happen by confessing to his part in whatever was going on.

The deputy said, "All this will be kept confidential. You go on runnin' your restaurant as if this meeting never took place. We're gatherin' evidence in the case and won't mention what you've told us until the criminals are in custody."

This interview sounded like a stroke of good fortune. Eric asked Hugh Fogel if he knew the persons at the meetings with Abe McDonnell. Fogel didn't know any names except a man named Frank who made reservations. No last name. One of the people involved paid the bill in cash. No credit cards. Eric sat disappointed with this ambiguity.

"Would you agree to have a forensic artist make a sketch of the people who came with Abe McDonnell?"

"Yeah. Sure. Just so's nobody knows about it."

The deputy said he would send an artist from the sheriff's office to try and capture images from Fogel's memory. "We got a good one at Malvern. She does a bang-up job."

Eric left the owner in the deputy's care. The steps to prove the involvement of Overshoot Mining in murder cases moved forward but at a painfully slow rate. "More of a shuffle than steps," he mused aloud.

The death of Abe's doctor and the nephew who died in the state park were next on Eric's list to investigate. *I want to know what chemical was fed to Abe McDonnell.* Fogel's statement proved useless here. He was clueless about the identity of the additive. Fogel firmly stated he had no direct involvement. One of the gang who came with Abe administered the chemical to his food or drink.

Time to give Sean McDonnell an update. Eric called McDonnell's office and caught him up to date on developments. Sean said, "Glad you've finally got witnesses who're alive. I wonder how helpful they'll be in the trial over the validity of Abe's will." He shook his head in disgust as Eric described the connection between Abe's poisoning and the exploding Jaguar. "We've got to find out what they're up to!"

"I'll look into that after I nail down the cause of Abe's death. There're too many leads to reach closure on any topic yet."

"I know. It's just that I wonder what's so important on Abe's property for people to be murdered."

"You and me both."

Their phone conversation ended, and Eric debated which apparent murder to follow up first. He had planned to check on the doctor's death to discover the lethal chemical fed to Abe. But he changed his mind and decided to focus instead on the death of Abe's nephew. How that might tie in could lead to another bit of evidence to convict somebody for murder. *I hope I'm not grasping at straws in the wind.*

Eric called Megan. "Any info on the death of Paul McDonnell?"

"You bet. I'm texting you what little there is about his "accident". I did find one source who might help. He's the investigating park ranger named Edwin Markey. Markey lives not far from other McDonnell family members."

"Thanks. I'll check with him. Any McDonnell's death is suspicious in my books."

These people all live in the Highlands! My poor sedan won't have any shocks left after these trips. Rural Arkansas potholes are second to none. The scenery makes up for a little of the rough ride. The ranger's home was surrounded by thick woods. Bird feeders hung from nearby trees. *Low-lying feeders must attract racoons, rabbits, and squirrels. This guy is a real naturalist.* Eric knocked on the ranger's door. A dark-haired man in his 40s with bright blue eyes gave a loud greeting.

"Howdy! What can I do for you, sir?"

"I'm Eric Bonfield, private investigator. I've got some questions about the death of Paul McDonnell. I understand you were the officer who found him."

"Oh, yes. What a tragedy. Come on in. If I can help, I want to."

The nicely decorated cottage was filled with evidence that a park ranger was in residence. Edwin liked to talk. He immediately began showing Eric his acquired collection of cat claw prints.

"These casts of footprints assist me in trackin' animals, especially exotic ones released in the park by unwitting citizens. I hope to use this information to trace what happens to non-native species on state park property. You'd be surprised how many pets get turned loose in our parks."

Eric couldn't see how this might be relevant to Paul McDonnell's death, but he let Edwin talk on and on. Eventually Eric broke into the one-sided conversation, "This is certainly an interesting subject. but I was wondering what you can tell me about the death of Paul McDonnell?"

Edwin didn't take any prodding to give his version of Paul's death. "I don't deal with many tragedies in this business. The things I experience usually involve people turnin' their ankles, breakin' a bone, or somethin' like that. In this state park there aren't many places where a person can get themselves killed unless they have help!"

"What do you mean by that?" Eric's face lit up.

"Let me tell you about Paul's death, and maybe it'll 'come clear what I'm sayin'. I was followin' a remote path through the park when I heard this scream. Sounded human and male. Sometimes it's hard to make out the direction of a noise in thick canopy, but finally I headed toward the sound. There weren't any more screams, but I heard somebody runnin' through the brush. This all sounded strange, so I kept lookin' for the source of the scream. At last I came to one of the rocky bluffs in the park. I looked down and saw a body lyin' at the base of the cliff. I walked down there to see what happened.

"By the time I got to Paul, it was too late. He died 'fore I found him. I radioed my superior. The crew he sent took two hours to reach the site. That tells you how remote it was. While I waited for the squad to arrive, I looked 'round the top of the bluff for clues. There were footprints, and I suppose you could say it looked like a scuffle. But, other than footprints, that's all I found. Because I love animal foot tracks, I wanted to interpret these human footprints in the soil."

"But the report called it an accident," said Eric.

"Yeah, I know. I told the investigators 'bout the runnin' person in the brush and 'bout the scream. But they said it was all circumstantial. They talked up the idea that an accident fit best with what they saw. In my opinion, they're worried 'bout bad publicity for the state park."

"Did you check out the footprints?"

"Yep. I made casts of the prints. I always carry materials with me in case I come across a set of animal imprints. I tracked the footprints until the brush was too thick to make progress. They seemed to go in the direction of the runnin' person I heard."

"What did the coroner have to say about cause of death?"

"This gets interestin'. She found bruise marks on Paul's body that couldn't be made by a simple fall. But it didn't convince investigators of anythin' but an accidental death. I think they goofed up. Like I said, too concerned with publicity. Who wants to hike in a park where somebody's murdered? Easier to call it an accident. Then ya can just tell people to watch out for steep slopes."

"Do you still have the footprint casts?"

"Yep. You want 'em?"

"I'd like to take them to a forensic specialist at the Pulaski County sheriff's office in Little Rock. You never know what might turn up. Is there anything else you can tell me?"

"Yeah," said Markey solemnly. "I knew Paul. He was a skilled hiker who loved to walk in this park. He knew trails others didn't know 'bout. For anybody but Paul to be on this particular path just didn't make sense."

"Thanks, Edwin. I'll take those prints now."

"Glad somebody is on this case. I felt uneasy 'bout the investigation from the start."

"You're an observant person. Most people would miss the clues you saw. And to make casts of the prints was a stroke of genius. I hope they lead to whoever was involved in Paul's death." *I especially hope this leads to the Overshoot gang.*

Before he left for Little Rock, Eric wanted to visit the office of Abe's murdered doctor. *Wait a minute! I'll bet the sheriff in Malvern has the information I need.* He walked into the office of the deputy in charge of investigating Paul McDonnell's death and the murder of Abe's doctor.

"Can I get a copy of the coroner's report detailing the bruises on Paul McDonnell's body and the analysis of a blood test done on Abe McDonnell by his doctor?"

"No problem here. As with all unsolved murder cases involving doctors, we keep every physician's files in secure storage. Never know what'll turn up."

"Great!" Eric scanned the computerized data. From Frances's detailed notes, Eric knew the date of Abe's blood draw."

The deputy said, "Them goons who did the doc in really ransacked his office and burned every record they could find. But the doc kept electronic files of all patient data. They must not have known 'bout this."

Abe's report easily popped up. Eric sent a copy to a forensic chemist friend of his.

In a few seconds the chemist called Eric. "Where'd you get this? There must be some mistake. I've never seen such a high concentration of this particular biochemical in somebody's blood—this is very serious."

"What kind of symptoms would one expect to have with this in their blood stream?"

"I suspect whoever ingested this couldn't think very well."

Eric pressed the issue. "If he continued to take it, what might happen?"

"This substance is toxic at low levels and, given enough time and exposure, could result in death."

"And I'm afraid that's exactly what happened. Thanks for help in solving this case."

"Glad to be of help."

To the deputy, Eric said, "Here's some important evidence related to the death of Abe McDonnell. If you could forward this stuff to Amy at the Pulaski County sheriff's forensics lab, I'd appreciate it."

"You got it!"

On the drive back to Little Rock, Eric felt better about the evidence. *It looks like we're getting closer to exposing Overshoot Mining's plan to grab Abe's mining rights.*

At the forensics lab, Amy inspected the footprint casts. Eric was amazed at what a well-preserved print can reveal. Besides Paul McDonnell's prints, the others belonged to a man with a size 10 shoe. The unique style was particularly telling. "Most hikers wear boots but not the owner of this impression," Amy said. "You don't find this brand in a typical shoe store. It's an expensive Italian model sold only in very upscale specialty shops. Why would anyone hike in such a remote area in a costly dress shoe?"

Eric's eyes widened. "Why indeed?" He took down all the information she could give him, thanked her profusely, and hurried to his office. He breathlessly burst into home base and said, "Megan, can you do a search of outlets for this particular shoe?"

Megan knew never to be surprised by Eric's requests. "Must be important. I'll get right on it. I assume you want exact locations?"

"You bet!"

She stopped working on routine filing to plunge into the murky world of exotic imported men's shoes. *Never thought I'd do shoe shopping for my boss!* She smiled and pushed "search".

Time to see Sean McDonnell. I think he'll be excited with the latest findings.

It was late afternoon when Eric entered McDonnell's bank. Just before he entered Sean's office, Megan called.

"Got what you wanted on that shoe. Turns out they only sell them in New York at one of the most expensive shoe shops in town. Your killer is an import. He should have a definite accent that doesn't match anyone native to Arkansas!"

"Megan, you're a dream! Thanks a lot."

"Can it, Eric. I just do my job." But she smiled as she hung up the phone.

He hurried into McDonnell's office with the evidence.

"Great stuff, Eric," said Sean. "But we still can't pin this on Overshoot Mining, or can we? We don't know this is the chemical these guys used to spike Abe's food. I know enough about crooked lawyers and how they can twist this around to appear circumstantial."

"You're right. I'm afraid we don't have that crucial bit of information. We need to find the men who brought Abe to the restaurant for his poisoned meal. The forensic artist may have sketches from the restaurant owner's memory drawn up by now. Then we can begin searching for likely suspects."

"Keep me posted," said Sean.

"Always."

Chapter 10

Eric stepped out of the office building where he and Sean McDonnell held counsel. To keep his promise of safety to Sarah, Eric quickly turned and moved to the side after taking a few steps. This movement saved his life. A bullet struck the building facing and ricocheted away from Eric. Concrete dust partially blinded him. He broke into a run but knew another bullet would soon come his way. Eric zig-zagged to make a difficult target. A second shot grazed the heel of Eric's right shoe. A third shot came so close to his head he felt the breeze of the bullet as it passed.

At last, Eric burst inside the building next door. He phoned police and gave the approximate direction where the shots came from. An abandoned office building on the opposite side of the street was a great place for an assassin to wait. Broken windows marked possible locations where a sniper could post while waiting for a victim.

He called Sean McDonnell, "Stay inside. There's a shooter out here." McDonnell asked if Eric was okay. "I'm fine, and I'm glad this building wasn't locked!"

Police arrived from all directions within minutes and surrounded the abandoned structure. A bystander observed Eric's frantic run and called police. It appeared the shooter couldn't escape, or so it seemed. *This person's a hired marksman. No professional killer will choose a place without an exit.*

Officers scoured the building. They found spent cartridge shells on the third floor. *Smart guy! Ideal trajectory for an accurate shot. Verifies the shooter is a professional.* Footprints in the dust showed the person's escape. A back stairway led to a tunnel which connected to other buildings. He made a clean getaway and left no DNA residue.

Eric asked the investigating team to make casts of the clearest footprints. He took these to Amy in forensics. *She can compare them with casts from the forest.*

Since Eric's car wasn't bombed, he had transportation. The day was nearly spent but looked like one of the best in this investigation. *I'm going to reward myself by enjoying an evening with my favorite brunette.* He punched her number into his cell phone.

"Hey, Sarah, how about a dinner date?"

"Sounds good; who with?" she teased.

"Oh, maybe somebody you know. Can he pick you up at 6:00?"

"Provided he has proper identification."

"He'll bring a birth certificate."

Eric brushed himself free of concrete dust and decided to clean up at his apartment. After a shower, his cell phone rang. It was Amy, the forensic specialist.

She announced, "Those casts the police brought over; they're a perfect match with the ones from the forest murder."

"Fantastic! That connects a couple dots in the mining case. Thanks!"

"Any time. Your stuff is my job insurance."

I wonder if this is also the other driver who escaped after he collided with his accomplice. Maybe we're closing in on someone. If police can identify the shooter and pin Paul McDonnell's death on him, he might squeal on who paid him to kill. From what Megan said, this guy is from New York, or at least shops there.

With his personal assassin on the loose, Eric took special caution. As he drove out of his apartment parking lot, he noticed an unfamiliar car. It might be someone in his building who traded in their old model for a new one. Then again, maybe something else was going on. *Better play it safe.* He speeded up as he left the lot. Watching in his rear-view mirror, he saw the car start up and begin to move. *Suspicion verified.* Eric made a set of quick turns to throw off the pursuer. This time he wanted the upper hand and didn't want to get boxed in again. The other car kept pace and Eric couldn't shake the tail.

As he cruised toward the police station, Eric decided to lay a trap for the person following him. The car kept a reasonable distance behind. Eric called for reinforcements. One of the officers he knew answered the call and responded quickly. They worked out a plan to try and catch the shooter at his own game. After several minutes, a police car tailed Eric's follower. The officer used an unmarked vehicle. On cue, Eric turned down a narrow alley. The pursuing car followed. Eric stopped at the end of the alley and turned his car sideways to block any escape. The police car closed the gap at the other end. *Got him trapped now!* Eric carried a bullhorn with him for just such occasions. He slowly got out of his car with Glock and bullhorn in hand.

Would this be the break he needed to capture a live criminal who could make the link to Overshoot Mining? *At last!* Eric shouted at the driver. "Get out of the car with your hands up."

The boxed-in car sat a moment with its motor running. The policeman turned on his spotlight to illuminate the tail's car in the darkness of the alley. Dark clouds and tall buildings permitted little light from the very late afternoon sun into the enclosed space.

Eric could see the man behind the wheel talking on his cell phone. Eric was almost close enough to make out the man's features. Then Eric saw a look of horror break on the man's face. A second later the car exploded in a ball of flame. The occupant was incinerated.

Eric fell flat on the pavement to avoid fragments of the car that filled the air. He held up the bullhorn to deflect debris. A piece of metal knocked the horn out of his hand and tore through his jacket, raking his right arm. When he looked up, he was in shock as he watched his witness go up in smoke, along with evidence in the car. The officer called fire personnel and moved his car out of the way so equipment could reach the flames. Firemen arrived and put out the last fire remaining on the smoking remains of the vehicle.

Eric found the officer and they talked about what happened. "I saw a frightened look on the man's face right before the explosion. The car was rigged for just such a situation. His employer knew sooner or later one of the hit men who knew the identity of the payoff person would bungle a job so badly that he might be captured. The frantic phone call triggered a radio-controlled response. Problem solved. When forensics gets DNA evidence on this guy, I'm fairly certain they'll find he's from the Northeast."

"I'm afraid you got it figured out. Too bad. Awful way to die. Wonder why they got him from so far away?"

"Maybe they wanted a real professional." Eric sighed deeply. *I can't believe how thorough these guys are. Their only problem is to hire thugs who get the job done. Glad they fail. But the body count is way too high. Any body count is bad. What'll it take to implicate Overshoot Mining? Better call Sarah. I'll be late and she'll be worried.*

Darkness fell long before Eric rolled onto Fran and Devon's driveway. *Oh, Sarah! What're my escapades doing to you. Is all this too much? Will she just give up and walk away?* The answer came running off the front deck.

"Oh, Eric, are you OK? I heard the report on my police scanner."

She practically fell into his arms while smothering him with kisses. *I guess she isn't running away!*

"I'm fine; but I've got a torn jacket and a scratch that needs somebody's attention."

"Where? Show me!"

They sat at their friends' kitchen table. Fran and Devon were out for the evening. Eric removed his shirt and she gasped at the gash in his arm. Hurriedly she gathered first aid supplies, cleaned his wound, applied antiseptic, and attached a bandage. He detailed the events of the evening as she cared for his injury. "I'll fix that tear in your jacket too," she said. "What if you go and grab some takeout while I mend this coat?"

"Sounds like a bargain to me!" He went to a Chinese drive-thru and selected something he knew she'd like. By the time he returned, Sarah had finished the repair job and held his jacket up for inspection. Eric looked at the garment and shook his head. "That's amazing! I can't tell anything happened. You're so talented. At the rate you're fixing my jackets I'll hire you full time!"

Sarah blushed lightly. "Is that an offer?"

He opened his mouth, but nothing came out. Eric was wide-eyed for a moment. Then sweat popped out of his forehead.

She smiled and took up the conversation. "You just sit down, and let's enjoy this fare. Would you offer grace?" This broke the awkward silence.

It had been so long since his stomach saw a meal that it wondered if Eric's mouth had forgotten one of its purposes. Halfway through their dinner, his phone chimed. Eric listened, thanked the caller, and hung up. "After the fire folk cooled down the burnt car, forensics retrieved enough of the body to find his shoes. They were scorched but the soles matched footprints in the dust of the abandoned building where he tried to take me out. And, of course, they matched footprints in the park where Paul McDonnell was murdered."

Sarah asked, "Who was this man?"

"DNA should answer the question. He can't be a run-of-the-mill variety of criminal. He was persistent and smart, at least in the ways of crime. Probably from New York."

Sarah joined in Eric's thoughts. "At least you know who's responsible for Paul's death and attempts on your life. But this doesn't tie the killer to Overshoot Mining, does it?"

"You're right there." Eric's mind drifted away from conversation with Sarah. After a few minutes he looked up and saw her idly stirring her Chinese noodles. *I could kick myself for ignoring her.* "Sarah, I'm sorry. I slid into my own little world."

"I called a counselor today and made an appointment for us to get started on our work with her."

Eric let out the breath he held tightly. Relieved, he said, "That's great! When do we start?"

"Next Monday after my work."

Eric quickly entered the date to his phone. *If only I could solve the case before our meeting. Wishful thinking that!*

After dessert the wall clock told Eric he needed rest. Seeing his eye movement, Sarah picked up his jacket and helped him into it while carefully avoiding his damaged arm. With her close to him, Eric detected the lovely fragrance of a perfume he didn't recognize. "I like what you're wearing tonight," he said.

She laughed. "It's just an old outfit that's comfortable." She stepped in front of him, paused, and laughed again. "Oh, you mean my perfume. Yes, I selected it with you in mind. It's called, *Don't Stay Away.*"

Now Eric chuckled, "I like it very much." And he kissed her on the forehead.

"Do you know something?" she asked. He shook his head, waiting. "I'd like to rename the perfume and call it *Stay with Me Always.*"

Eric wished to sweep her into his arms, but his right arm denied this pleasure, and he didn't want to destroy her first aid work. Instead, he kissed her healing hand twice. "Thank you for repairing this body." Then he looked into her glistening eyes and said quietly, "I want to stay with you always."

She closed her eyes and said, "Oh, how I wish that was now!"

"Sorry. Time to go, but," he teased, "I might come back!"

Sarah almost punched his arm, but she remembered the gash and stopped in mid-air. "You're lucky you've got that problem with your arm, or I might smash you a good one!"

"Yeah, I guess an exploding car has some value." He tickled her. This brought a loud cry and she whacked his other arm. They both laughed until their sides ached.

As he left, she walked to her borrowed bedroom. *I wonder what it would be like to undress in front of Eric on our wedding night.* Then she caught herself. *Better hold that thought for later. Don't get your hopes up yet. Counseling might hold a stinger we haven't thought about.*

Chapter 11

As he drove into his parking lot, Eric did a quick scan. Nothing seemed out of place. *Good. I can use a reprieve from people trying to shoot me.* Then his mind shifted. *If I make a commitment to a woman, it'll be for "better or worse.* He paused and took a deep breath. *That sounds scary.* At this he shivered and twisted his shoulders. *Ouch! That gash stings! Better see Alice and make certain my bandages are okay.*

Alice was at work, so he carefully did his own first aid check on the arm.

The next morning turned windy and rainy. Eric didn't dress in haste. He took the time to fix a decent breakfast. Fast food often dominated his lifestyle during the day, or he skipped meals, like he did yesterday. All that fat and high calorie stuff didn't fit anybody's good health plan. Eating with Sarah, he tended to make better food choices.

He found Alice and asked for a bandage check.

"What did I tell you about avoiding bullets?"

"I know, I know. But this wasn't done by a bullet."

"Excuses, excuses." Alice had a good sense of humor. "If you keep this up, I'm going to have to charge you full rate."

"Any charge wouldn't be enough. You do great work."

In the parking lot, he did his usual car check and found nothing suspicious. But, to be extra cautious and partly to please Sarah, he used the remote starter from a relatively safe distance. Nothing greeted him but the sound of an ancient internal combustion engine starting, after making a few complaints. He drove leisurely to the office and parked in a conspicuous place to discourage would-be saboteurs. Megan greeted him with her pleasant smile and handed him a pile of work. *She is so efficient!*

"So, tell me about yesterday. I see you dodged another piece of shrapnel while you gathered evidence."

He outlined the details and thanked her for her work on the criminal's shoes. "Anything from the police today?"

"Yes, you'll find it right on top. Seems DNA evidence of the guy with the Italian shoes places him in New York. He's wanted for some pretty classy crimes."

"I guess so!" said Eric, after reading the list of grisly things the person accomplished.

"And to think you had a hand in almost capturing him!"

"The word 'almost' is the kicker," said Eric. "I wish I could find the perpetrator or perpetrators behind all this mayhem. Every time I'm about to get a break, somebody who might have incriminating evidence ends up dead or unconscious. I'd better call the hospitals to see if those guys have given any helpful information."

"Already did," said Megan. "No such luck. All have talked and everyone was hired by phone and couldn't give any helpful identification about their employer."

"Thanks." He sighed.

Eric mindlessly trudged through routine reports. He loved what he did, but this Overshoot thing bugged him. As his mind wandered, his partner came in. "Hey, Joseph, how're things coming on your end?"

Joseph was excited, something unusual for such a mild-mannered man. He took most of life in stride. Joseph liked to keep his emotions in check, so he could think objectively. "My friend, I just got the results from the 'problem' water well. There're some very odd chemicals in the groundwater. They're complex organic compounds that range from having an obnoxious odor to some that're extremely lethal. I see why the farmer was so concerned."

"Excellent!" said Eric. "Where exactly is the well?"

They crowded around a county map and located the farm with the contaminated well water. It sat less than a quarter mile from Abe McConnell's farm. Bells began to ring in Eric's head. *Could this be the reason why the Overshoot mining folk remain so secretive about their operation?* "Joseph, this reminds me of the contaminated wells on Sarah's farm involving that fake oil company. Maybe this is a repeat case. Of course, contamination can be circumstantial. It might not be related to Abe's farm and the mine. Do we have any idea where these organic compounds originate?"

"The lab said there were so many that it might be hard to pinpoint a single source."

Eric thought back to his organic chemistry class at the University of Arkansas. This list of analyzed chemicals was not tightly focused. *Many different industries could be responsible for creating this mess. It looks like a potluck supper with lots of contributors. That makes things complicated.* "How do we find where this stuff comes from?"

Joseph shook his head. "Got any ideas?"

Reflecting, Eric said, "That'll be tough. Instead, let's focus first on verifying that the mine is leaking out this stuff. Joseph, could you check with other farmers to see if they'll let you sample their water wells?"

"That'll take time. This county has many small farms," said Joseph.

"Let's focus on farms just around Abe's place."

Eric helped Joseph gather sampling supplies and load them into his car. Joseph had a plat map of the area to help him locate critical wells. As Eric watched Joseph drive away, he said to Megan, "There goes one of the most efficient people I know. We're fortunate to have him on board."

"Got that right!" echoed Megan.

"Now, I've got to do some serious geology." *I must know the exact nature of the permeable layers of rock that could feed chemicals to this polluted well.* To narrow possible sources meant a visit to the Arkansas Geological Survey. Eric knew most of the geologists there and trusted their expertise to provide solid answers, if any could be found.

Eric gathered his own materials and headed to the Survey. Located not far from the University of Arkansas at Little Rock, the survey was near the edge of a slightly wooded area. The front office secretary knew Eric.

"Hey, I hear you been gettin' some serious crime work in these days!"

"Yeah. Never knew geology and crime could go so well together." He laughed.

"Who ya want to see?"

"I need to see the Chief Stratigrapher, Alec Collins. Is he in?"

"You're in luck. Alec just got back from a conference."

Alec Collins' office resembled a museum of specimens collected from all over the state. Eric stared at the massive array of rocks, minerals, and fossils. "Alec, did you find all of these yourself?"

"Nah. Just maybe 80% or so. Some were brought in by interested citizens or other geologists. What can I do for you? I hope its related to some of the cool stuff you've been doin' in your detective work."

"You're in luck! I'm interested in the strata right around this location (he gave Alec the coordinates of Abe's farm). What can you tell me about permeable rocks there?"

After an hour of looking over maps of the region, Alec and Eric concluded that several underground aquifers could supply water to the farms around Abe's property. The geology in this part of the Ouachita Mountains is far more complicated than on the Coastal Plain where Sarah's farm sits.

"Thanks for the info, Alec. This is a big help." They shook hands.

"I'd love to do what you do. It sounds so interesting."

Eric pointed to three places on his body. "These are all going to make nice scars that tell part of the tale of just how exciting my work can be. Not certain you'd enjoy some of my experiences." They both laughed.

Eric made copies of Survey maps to help him trace the chemical sources of the farm's water well problem. The Survey's online water well database told of well depths in the vicinity of Abe's farm. *This could help narrow the list of possible shallow aquifers connecting to the mine.* He needed an airtight case against Overshoot Mining as the polluter.

Sitting in his car outside the Survey, Eric called Joseph. "While you're at it, can you take samples from any water wells on Abe's place? I know this might be dangerous, what with the Overshoot guards lurking around the farm."

"I'll be careful."

What other pieces of the puzzle are missing? He phoned the sheriff's office in Little Rock and asked if they had any success locating the men in the sketches from the restaurant owner's memory. The Hot Spring sheriff's forensic artist had forwarded her sketches to area law enforcement folk.

"There're several suspects who showed up on our search of databases, but identification remains elusive. I'm afraid the restaurant owner didn't have a very good memory," said Sheriff Hanson.

"Mind if I check out some of the suspects?"

"Go for it! I've only got so much manpower to devote to this."

Eric's status as a privileged P.I. permitted him to do investigative work beyond that of most private detectives. He'd earned this through his many successful closures of difficult cases that eluded law enforcement staff.

He downloaded the list and a sketch of the suspects to his cell phone. *Hugh Fogel's memory must be weak. These sketches don't show many identifying characteristics.* To check if any of the suspects on the sheriff's list had links to Overshoot Mining, Eric called Megan to work up composites on these people. *This might help or be a waste of time. I've got to start somewhere.* Megan started her methodical search. If information on these people existed, she would find it.

"Now that you've got the identity of the guy with the fancy shoes, I'll see what I can do about these people."

It'll take her a bit of time to find that data, so I'd better bring Sean McDonnell up to speed while I wait. Eric could always find McDonnell; he seemed to live in the bank's office building. *Did this man ever go home?* The secretary smiled and waved Eric into McDonnell's office. The banker listened to what Eric uncovered.

"So far, hard evidence remains in the meager category. My attorneys are pouring over the old will, the new will and contract, and the notarized sheet Josephine left, as well as her diary. The lawyers say they need more evidence to prepare a strong case against Overshoot Mining."

"Maybe I have something that might help," said Eric. He told Sean about Frances and her notarized notebook, as well as observations she and her brother made at the signing of the documents.

"I'll put my attorneys to work on these new sources. I don't know if these unprofessional observers at the signing constitute much evidence. We need professional witnesses who can testify about Abe's condition. This isn't an iron clad case."

"Agreed." Eric excused himself to work up the geology of the area around Abe's farm.

Sean experienced no threats. *Unlike me who stumbles into danger on a regular basis. Guess that's why he pays me the big bucks.* He laughed.

Exiting McDonnell's building and glancing around, Eric tried to catch the glint of any sniper's rifle. None showed. *Has Overshoot Mining run low on people to do the dirty work?* Eric chuckled as he approached his car. He stiffened when he saw signs of a jimmied door. Eric called the police bomb squad and asked for help. They arrived and searched the car but found nothing. It might be the work of a juvenile with time on his or her hands. Eric thanked the police and drove back to his office. *Maybe I'm too jumpy. Surely this company is running out of criminals to hire!*

At his office, Eric couldn't help but look over Megan's shoulder as she worked. She chided him for this and sent him to work on his geology project. "I can't concentrate on these databases with you hovering around!" This was said with a sly grin. Megan liked to give Eric static whenever she could. *He's too serious. Got to keep him loose.*

Eric backed off and busily dug into geologic data on the site. He used a three-dimensional mapping program to locate wells and strata that might connect to the Overshoot mine. He pulled data from many sources and loaded it into the mapping project. At least temporarily, this kept him out of Megan's hair.

After an hour, Megan announced that she found several names worth pursuing. Whether any of them might be the mysterious persons in the sketches derived from the restaurant owner's memory remained to be seen.

Eric studied the list. The database generated suspects from all walks of life. Eric prioritized the order of interviewees in his mind. Like an old-fashioned door-to-door salesman, he might knock on lots of doors before making a sale. He also knew that some prospects looked more promising than others. He entered the addresses in his GPS and headed out. Lots of dead ends lay ahead. *Oops! I want to avoid "dead" ones!*

The first individual on the list lived on the north side of town. Eric hoped to catch the suspect off guard.

Suzie barked out directions and turns from his GPS unit.

A rundown house in an equally rundown neighborhood greeted him. Eric got out of his car, locked it, and quickly walked to the front door. He glanced around as he did. His loaded Glock created a bulge in his jacket. He didn't want to use it, but one never knew what to expect. The Overshoot gang had no compunctions about killing people.

He knocked on the door. It rattled as his knuckles rapped three times. After a couple minutes, the door opened slightly, and a tired looking elderly woman with streaked, grayish hair peeked under the door chain. "Whadda ya want?"

"Excuse me, ma'am, but I'm looking for Mr. Waldo Essex. Would he live here?"

"Waldo moved outta here last week . . . permanently, if ya know what I mean?"

"Do you mean he is deceased?"

"Dead; that's what he is. Drank too much, smoked like a factory, and wouldn't work. Never left this house in the last year. Miserable man, he was."

"I'm sorry to have bothered you. You've given me all the information I need."

Eric turned and left rapidly. *That was creepy. I'd better make certain Waldo is deceased. If that woman told the truth, he couldn't be the man I'm after.* He texted the information to Megan for verification.

The second person on the list lived not far away in a more expensive neighborhood. Sparkling clean BMWs lay out for display on several driveways. This spoke volumes. And these two neighborhoods were so close to each other. *Equality of income hasn't hit Little Rock. No different than the rest of the country.* A knock at the door brought a teenage girl. "Yeah? What's up?"

"I'd like to speak with Mr. Jeffrey Stanky. Is he in?"

"Never home. Always in New York or Los Angeles on business. What ya want him for?"

"I'm a private investigator (obligatory creds shown) and have a few questions."

"Private eye, are ya? Well, if ya can find him, you'll do better than us. Sends us money but won't give us the time of day!"

"You wouldn't happen to know where he was last week, would you?"

"Called from some place in New Jersey, I think. Nah, he don't like Little Rock. Won't catch him here!"

Eric thanked the teen. Her information probably eliminated Mr. Stanky from Eric's prospect list. Two strikes on the list so far. Eric called Megan and relayed the information. He asked her to check on this alibi too.

While she was on the phone, Megan gave him additional names and addresses. Eric dutifully plodded through the list. Each person seemed less and less like the men Eric sought. After checking alibis and shortening the list, Eric's hopes began to dwindle.

He was tired and needed some lunch. The list had taken him to the west and into the Highlands again. *Since I'm here, might as well eat at the restaurant where this all started with a bang!* The road's potholes hadn't improved. This restaurant's rural setting suited Eric more than sterile city cafes and eateries that dotted the area near his office. He felt uncomfortable in the noisy bustle of such places. Although hardly an extreme introvert, he enjoyed solitude now and then.

Rolling hills and valleys appealed to him far more than the crowded downtown. Driving through areas with real rock outcrops pulled his mind away from corporate gangsters and murder. At a particularly well-exposed rock exposure, Eric placed the visible structure on his mental geologic map of Arkansas. Having seen thousands of rock outcrops in his professional life, he made a reasonable guess as to how this one fit into the geology of his home state. Such a distraction had a calming effect on an otherwise discouraging morning.

The by-now-familiar restaurant loomed ahead. News of the owner's testimony about the gang who fed Abe his deadly cocktail must not have leaked out. Business was brisk from the looks of the parking lot.

Chapter 12

The vast number of vehicles in the parking lot were pickups. *Wish my pickup was fixed by now.* Eric placed his car in full view of a large window. *I don't want to take any chances.*

Inside, he caught the eye of the waiter who gave him the dropped magnetite and asked about the lunch special.

"Yir that detective, right? Got the bomber of the boss's Jag yet?"

"Sorry, I can't comment on an ongoing investigation. But we're on the case."

Eric took in the large dining area while he waited for food to arrive. *Did I miss anything when I was here earlier?* The spacious serving room looked as he remembered it. His eyes took in details about the room. It was plain, but clean. Wall hangings were tastefully arranged. *I wonder who plans his décor?* As his gaze scanned the walls, he saw something for the first time. A very small window, almost invisible to the casual observer, overlooked the dining room. *What could that be?*

Since his food was taking its time arriving, Eric strolled to the window. Obviously one-way glass, it permitted viewing only from the other side of the wall. He casually ambled around and found an unlocked door. Eric stepped into a small room with a video camera, sound recording system, still camera, computer, color laser printer, and the other side of the one-way glass window! *This is fascinating.* Peeking through the window he saw clearly every part of the dining room. *Photography from here would be easy. What's the owner up to?* Eric slipped out and returned to his seat in time for his sandwich and drink to arrive.

After eating and paying for the meal, Eric walked directly to the owner's office. *Got to know what's up with all the secret photography.* Eric knocked on Fogel's door. The man sat at his desk nursing a cigar that he never lighted. He looked up when Eric entered. Obviously surprised, he said, "So, Mr. Private Detective. What can I do for ya today?"

"I was wondering why you have such an elaborate photography studio hidden behind a one-way window."

Eric got the most information from Hugh Fogel by not allowing him time to generate tall tales.

"How . . . how . . ."

"Look, let's not start that again. You run a shady establishment here, and I want to know what's going on."

The man's defenses fell apart. Crestfallen, Fogel told Eric certain clientele wanted video and audio recordings of their breakfast, lunch, or dinner meetings but without everyone knowing it was happening.

Eric despised such arrangements. "And did you illegally record the conversations of Abe McDonnell and his companion or companions?"

Trying to be composed, Fogel said, "Yeah, I did. But I keep all the old DVDs in a safe in this office, and nobody has access but me."

"Can you produce those? They may be important in the investigation of Abe McDonnell's death." Reluctantly, Fogel got up from his chair and bent over the safe. After a few turns of the knob, the safe door opened, and a stack of computer discs showed themselves. Eric had called the sheriff's office in Malvern after discovering the hidden photo shop. A deputy entered as the DVDs exited the safe and ended up on the desk. Fogel seemed all too willing to get rid of the discs. The officer officially confiscated the evidence, gave the owner a receipt for the goods, and agreed to have them sent to Little Rock, to be added to a growing collection of evidence in the Pulaski County sheriff's evidence lockup.

The deputy asked Fogel if he would agree to a filmed interview. Fogel seemed so relieved to get out from under the cloud that hovered over his involvement in the coverup that he readily signed a document permitting the filming.

Hugh Fogel began his interview by describing his first contact with the people who brought Abe McDonnell to the restaurant. He revealed much more information than the first time Eric confronted him. Fogel seemed willing to talk, since the DVD recordings could easily be used against him. He might lose his business over this fiasco, or worse.

From Fogel's testimony, it was clear the setup for Abe was designed to gather as much information as possible. The people with him seemed desperate to cover all bases and wanted every conversation recorded and filmed. *These guys must be ignorant of the law or whatever. I can't imagine why they'd need this since it couldn't be presented in court. Something this illegal would never be of any legal value to benefit the Overshoot group. Maybe they wanted to show the recordings to Abe to prove that he said something he later denied.*

"Did you give these people copies of your recordings?"

"No, they must've realized all this filmin' was worthless. Besides, Abe never seemed enthusiastic to agree to their demands."

"So, there were no documents signed in your restaurant?"

"None. These people were disappointed. But they paid me and said they couldn't care less about the DVDs. I doubt they figured I'd keep 'em."

Interesting. They never got Abe's signature and were frustrated meeting here. Hence signatures were only done at his home when he was too ill to resist. Leaving the recordings here just might be Overshoot Mining's first wrong move. Those recordings and Fogel's testimony might be good evidence that Overshoot Mining lacks credibility. They might also prove that Abe never wanted to sign any of their phony documents. Now the law had these recordings and a witness tying them to, I hope, Overshoot Mining. Eric felt better. This, together with the witness of Frances and Eddy, who saw the way Overshoot Mining forced Abe to sign the will, might be the fracture needed to crack open the case.

Eric's notebook ran over. *Better get a new one.* The restaurant stood empty by the conclusion of the interview. Customers tended to cluster around traditional mealtimes, so wait staff lounged in a far corner of the dining area as they played cards.

The deputy took the DVD recordings and camera to his vehicle. Eric stayed long enough to thank Fogel and put the recording of his testimony in a sealed container. The deputy's car was at the far end of the restaurant parking lot. Eric exited the restaurant with Fogel's testimony in hand. Eric's car was at the front of the lot. As he approached it, a man with a gun appeared.

"OK, mister. Git in yir car an' close da door." Eric did as instructed. "Now, I'll jist take what's in yir hand."

As the thug reached to grab the recording, Eric quickly tossed the package onto the back seat. The man turned to retrieve it which caused the gun to point away from Eric. Eric grabbed the man's gun hand and smashed it against the steering wheel. A sharp report filled the car with a sound that temporarily deafened them both. The bullet shattered a side window.

They wrestled over the gun. The man was strong, but Eric's workouts proved him stronger. Even with his injured arm, Eric managed to wrest the gun out of the criminal's grasp. Once the gun dropped to the floor, Eric punched the man in the nose. An eruption of blood spattered them both. Before Eric could follow up his advantage, the man leaped from the car. As he did, he grabbed a grenade from his pocket, pulled the pin, and tossed the weapon onto the rear seat.

Eric jumped from the car and slammed the door as a shield from the upcoming blast. He stumbled as fast as he could to the nearest car and fell behind it. A few moments later, an explosion destroyed the inside of Eric's rental. He moved further away in case the fuel tank should blow. It did not. As car debris settled, Eric saw the mugger's car screeching away, leaving tire marks on the blacktop.

The sheriff's deputy came running from the far end of the lot, but the criminal was gone. Eric shook his head. Perhaps Overshoot Mining might be slightly ahead for now. *The recording is toast, but I'm still alive.* Eric gave the deputy a description of the assailant and his car.

So many bad guys coming to Arkansas; but why? What's so important on Abe's property to warrant murder? Then he stopped, eyes wide, as he realized how things could play out. *If they were onto the recording, they knew Fogel squealed on them.* Eric ran toward the building. He shot past gawking wait staff who assembled to inspect his wrecked car; it looked like a fugitive from a war zone.

Hugh Fogel dashed to his car. Eric shouted for him to stop, but it was too late. As Fogel opened the car door, the vehicle erupted in an explosion much greater than the grenade tossed into Eric's rental. Eric ducked behind the nearest pickup as pieces of metal and plastic battered the landscape. Restaurant staff fell or jumped behind pickups to shield themselves from the blast.

As Eric stood and surveyed the chaos, he shook his head. *Why this senseless barbarism? I'd just talked with Fogel, and now the man's in pieces. What'll stop this stupidity?*

Numbness took over Eric. He was a mess, splattered with the criminal's blood mixed with dirt blown onto him by the two blasts. He tried to pray, but his mind was too confused to even think. *What'm I supposed to do?*

He sat on the steps of the restaurant and gazed with incredulity. Eric remembered something he learned in Sunday school as a child. *"When you don't know what to do, you are probably pushing too hard. Let go of your problem and give it to God." That sounded so easy and trite. But I can't let go of something that takes the lives of so many people.* He thought of Hugh Fogel. *Was Fogel a criminal? The question is moot. Courts will never prosecute him. Overshoot Mining saw to that.*

Eric's mind began to clear a little, and he realized that letting go of a problem didn't mean giving up on it. *The shooter achieved two of three assignments. Fogel is dead and his recorded testimony is destroyed.* Only Eric could be considered a failed assignment. *I'm alive.* Plus, we have the DVDs! That's a plus the Overshoot people may not be aware of. He bit his lip. *I guess I've got to see this mess to the end, whatever that means.* A key witness was lost in the latest violence. *At this rate, it feels like the whole county's going to end up in the hospital or the morgue.*

Additional sheriff deputies arrived to survey the destruction and take testimonies from bystanders. Firefighters extinguished the blaze and EMT personnel checked for injuries. No serious problems.

After giving his narration of events to deputies, Eric called the car rental company. They were on a first name basis. "Yes, we can deliver yet another car. It'll take a bit to reach the restaurant."

"You don't know how much I appreciate your patience. I really don't try to destroy your cars."

"Got it. If you don't mind older models. We decided to keep a stock of these just for you." The agent chuckled.

"Glad to receive such excellent service!" Eric joined in the laugh.

Where do they find all their patience? I know they'll never trust me with nice, well-maintained vehicles. Eric smiled and mumbled, "Older models? Right. The destroyed-car business is booming in central Arkansas." *Yes, "booming" isn't a bad description.* While he waited for a car, Eric called Sarah and told her, "I'm fine."

"Since when does 'fine' mean wrestling with a criminal waving a gun and almost being blown up?" she said with a shaky voice. Sarah had listened to early chatter on police radio and guessed Eric was in the middle of this excitement.

He rubbed his temples. *It's getting harder and harder to reassure Sarah that I'm trying to stay safe.* He escaped death again today. *How many times can I do this hat trick?* He did his best to calm Sarah and told her they could have dinner anywhere she chose.

"I don't care where we meet; I just want you in one piece!"

"That's my number one goal!"

"It better be!" Sarah sobbed.

Eric was running out of encouraging things to say to her. So, he ended the conversation with, "I love you."

After making reservations, Eric called Megan to fill her in on the case.

"Did you get a good enough look at this guy to see if he's one in Fogel's sketches?"

"Doesn't match any of the sketches." He paused. "Killers for hire seem to be easy to find. Overshoot probably considers them expendable. Plus, he didn't strike me as a lawyer or administrative type. I hate to ask, but do you have any other people I can visit who match the sketches?"

"Just one."

"Guess I'll try that one," Eric wearily told Megan.

The rental car finally arrived, and Eric signed the papers. The agent noted Eric's blood-spattered face and clothes and asked, "Are you okay?"

"Physically? I'm fine. But that's about it."

"You sure are rough on our cars. Hope you don't have anything against us."

Eric told the young woman he had no vendetta against the agency. A clunker would do just fine. She grinned and handed Eric the keys to a freshly detailed, ten-year old model.

"And, yes, it has a remote starter." She smiled and walked to her partner's vehicle.

Eric thanked her and drove to his apartment. On the way, he stopped by the sheriff's office in Little Rock and gave Amy his jacket to check the blood stains and other marks for possible identification.

"You look a mess, if you don't mind me saying so." She smiled.

"And I feel that way too. I'm headed to correct this impression." He laughed weakly.

"I'll see what I can do about DNA."

"You do great work!"

"Yeah, whatever!" She smiled.

A change of clothes and shower helped Eric mentally prepare to visit the last person on Megan's list. *I really want to look at those recordings in the sheriff's security locker. Sean's attorneys need to have easy access to this evidence. Time is more important than ever now. The murders must stop. Sean's court date for a preliminary hearing won't wait. I need more evidence for his attorneys. Got to crack this case and move on with my life.*

Chapter 13

It was late when Eric found his last prospect. He resided in a deeply wooded area in a Little Rock suburb far from prying eyes. *Even hard to find the address! Suzie had to work for this location.* The man who came to the door was wary. "I'm looking for Mr. James Watson," Eric said.

"That would be me," said the man. Watson was a thin man with wrinkled skin, deep-set eyes, and a suspicious frown.

Eric's creds helped to admit him inside. The interior held no candle to anything he had viewed during the last several days. A living room sported ornate furniture and figurines.

"I love your decorations," Eric said. The place had a roomy and pleasant feel. When he had a good look at Mr. Watson, Eric felt disappointed. Watson didn't seem to match any of the sketched images, but Eric decided to ask a few questions just to be certain. His last question hit pay dirt.

"Mr. Watson, do you know anyone at Overshoot Mining?"

The man turned almost white and began to stammer. Eric knew he'd touched a sore spot. He pressed on. "What do you know about their operation?" More stammering and a look of confusion. "Apparently you do know about this company. I need to know all you can tell me." Eric's eyes bored into James Watson like a drill and the man fidgeted in his chair.

Finally, he found his tongue. "I used to work for them."

"What did you do in their employ?"

"I was a paralegal. I helped their law office with contracts and such."

Bingo! Eric had stumbled onto a potential gold mine. "Do you remember handling a contract and will for one Abe McDonnell?"

More stammering. Finally, he said, "Yes, I wrote those up for one of the lawyers."

Eric's blood raced. "Did you ever attend meetings at a restaurant with Mr. McDonnell?"

"Yes, I did. I always felt awkward. Mr. McDonnell didn't cooperate at all. But he did like the food."

Fogel's sketches were way off from reality! Either that or Watson's been through the wars since those food events. Or maybe Fogel tried to throw everybody off the scent.

"Were you present when Abe signed the contract and will at his home?"

"Yes, I saw him sign them both."

Eric continued to press. "Was Mr. McDonnell in full control of his faculties when he signed these documents?"

"'I have to say he didn't appear to be. He looked confused and weak when he signed the contract. Things were much worse on the day Abe signed the will. He seemed almost ready to die. But my boss pressed the issue. McDonnell finally signed the will."

"To be clear, you prepared the contract and will?"

"Yes, and I felt dirty for doing it. The document that replaced Abe's original will totally cut out any relatives from the mine's proceeds."

Eric was frantically taking notes. "What was the lawyer's name?"

"Sam Beechtree."

"Did you observe anyone spiking Abe's food or drink during these meetings?"

"Yes. Beechtree was very careful so no one would notice, but I'm certain he's the one who added something to Abe's drinks. I had no idea what it was but became suspicious that it wasn't a good thing."

Eric played his top card. "Would you testify in court to what you've told me?"

Watson hesitated, but finally agreed it would be the right thing to do. Eric breathed a sigh of relief at this breakthrough. *Now, if I can only keep this man alive until the trial!*

Watson emphasized he no longer worked for Overshoot Mining. His position terminated after the Abe McDonnell fiasco.

"I now work for another law firm in Little Rock."

Eric suggested that Watson should go about his life as if this conversation never occurred. He might be contacted later by Sean McDonnell's attorney if his testimony would help.

Watson wiped his forehead with a Kleenex. "I hope my testimony will straighten out something that I know was wrong."

On the way to Watson's house, Eric had used great care to avoid being tailed. He used similar caution going back to town. No one appeared to follow him.

As he drove, Eric became concerned about the usefulness of Watson's testimony in court. *Watson isn't a psychologist. He can't legally judge the mental ability of Abe when the contract and will were signed, or can he? Arkansas law is a bit ambiguous at this point, but if Abe wasn't in charge of his mental facilities, the signature on the will meant nothing. Watson's testimony might help, but it may not be enough. As a witness, Watson might fare no better than Frances and her brother. But together could all three tip the scales?*

Eric's portfolio lacked the conclusive evidence he knew might nullify the contract and will. *Nothing is iron-clad; a few pieces don't make a full puzzle. Watson's testimony about Beechtree spiking Abe's drink should be enough to move toward a murder charge, but there was no evidence what was in the spike. We know what was in Abe's blood. Isn't that enough? Probably not.*

Eric decided on a new strategy to be safe. *I need to catch somebody who might try to booby trap my car.* He set up a video camera on the roof of his apartment and connected it to a recorder in his room. This provided a wide view of the parking lot where his car rested between events. Maybe he could identify someone tampering with his vehicle. After his video stakeout stood ready, he turned on the camera and got ready to see Sarah. Before going out, Eric quickly surveyed the recording. The car was clean. He drove to Sarah's farm. She had moved back in after forensics personnel and workers finished with her damaged house.

He escorted Sarah to his ramshackle vehicle. After apologizing for a less than exciting chariot, he drove them to an upscale restaurant. He couldn't use his camera setup there but tipped the attendant to keep an eye on the car. Eric smiled at what might be going through the attendant's mind. Most people who want their cars watched have expensive vehicles. *Mine doesn't fit that category!*

Although Sarah looked great, she wasn't her usual chatty self. She seemed only a little recovered from the shock of learning about Eric's most recent close calls. "How near are you to finishing this project? I'm rattled by what you experienced today! I still wonder if you don't need someone to guard you."

Eric had enough ego to dodge her suggestion. "I'm trying to be as safe as possible. It just seems that a new curve comes my way with each step forward. But I even have a video setup at my apartment to catch anyone tampering with my car."

"Thanks for trying to be safe. If only you had someone to watch your back."

"I'm doing as much as I can without crawling into a hole." He grinned, hoping for a response.

"Are you making fun of my suggestion?"

"Oh, no! Not at all. I just mean I can't solve this case without being exposed to danger. I promise to be safe." *If only I can keep this promise!*

His phone buzzed. After listening to the call, Eric returned to their table. "Amy's gone over some of Fogel's recordings and verified two people usually accompanied Abe at the restaurant meetings. I can't wait to identify Watson and Beechtree as people in the videos. I'll do this first thing in the morning." *What about the poisoning? Would videos show who contaminated Abe's drink?*

After he took Sarah home, Eric was excited about viewing the videos. *Maybe there'll be closure tomorrow.* He pulled into his parking lot thinking about bringing the Overshoot Mining gang to justice.

The lights guarding the lot were all out. Immediately, Eric's senses turned on alert. *Why so dark?* Hall lights burned in the apartment complex. It wasn't an electrical blackout. *Not looking good.* Scanning the lot with the beams of his headlights, Eric felt all his internal warning systems activate. The lights never went out in his parking lot because a backup system kicked in when power failed.

Eric spun the car around to leave the lot but found a large car blocking his way. *Why didn't I see that car following me? I was spaced out thinking about closing this case. My mistake!* He had the police on speed dial and punched the key. One of his friends on the force answered. Eric called for help. "Hurry!"

A patrol car cruised only six blocks away and would arrive in minutes. *Got to buy time so the cops can get here.* He pulled back into the lot and drove through open lanes. A bullet crashed through a side window and narrowly missed Eric's face. He sped up and looped around the lot. He tried to put other cars between himself and the direction the shot came from.

Eric judged the shot didn't come from the blocking car but from the opposite side of the parking area. *Smart. They're covering the lot from opposing directions. I'm caught in a crossfire! How can I take advantage of this trap?*

A thought came to him halfway down one side of the lot. He stopped the car quickly, opened the door, and slid onto the pavement. Shots rang from both directions. *Good! Keep it up.* He knifed his way between cars, keeping low. More shots. When he reached the middle of the lot, he quickly raised his Glock and fired in the general direction of one of the shots. This brought a volley of rounds from both sides of the trap. A cry came from the car blocking the lot. As he hoped, direct crossfire wounded one of the men. No more shots.

The familiar whine of a police car siren and flashing lights converged on the lot. Eric heard feet running. A person headed right past Eric's position. With only the light available from Eric's car and the oncoming police vehicle, Eric could just make out the man moving past him.

Eric lunged for the man's legs and knocked him to the ground. A gun clattered to the pavement. Eric grabbed the man's arm and twisted it to his back as he held him against the pavement. Handcuffs were rapidly applied as the man screamed obscenities. Although Eric's wounds hurt, he held tightly to the thug. Meanwhile, police stopped beside the other man's car, and one of the officers checked the downed man. The other officer called for an ambulance. Eric pulled the protesting man toward the policeman who stood by the fallen criminal. "I suggest a formal arrest," said Eric.

The officer pointed to the man on the ground and said, "We've got a badly wounded man on our hands, Eric, do you have an explanation?"

"Yes, I do. I think this struggling gentleman is the shooter."

At that point the man began to protest. He claimed the shooting was an accident.

"And was your firing a weapon an accident?" asked the officer sarcastically.

This guy wasn't the sharpest tool in Overshoot's box. He began to spill information. The man waived his rights and proceeded to disgorge data like a computer. Unfortunately, most of it was gibberish.

Eric hoped this person could be connected directly to Overshoot Mining. However, as other captured criminals claimed, an intermediary served as buffer. Hired gunmen never knew the name of their real employer. The intermediary was "Jimmie"; no last name. The only contact with "Jimmie" was by phone. Payment came in a post office box. "Jimmie" was the same name one of the men gave Eric after being shot in Sarah's bedroom.

An ambulance arrived and carried the injured man to a local hospital. A guard was assigned to the door. The uninjured man was carted to jail. Eric called the night number of the car rental company and informed them their car would need a new side window.

"Is that it? Nothing else needs repair?" The operator laughed. She had taken most of Eric's calls for replacing rentals.

"Yep, this time I avoided an explosion or other type of total destruction." Eric replied with as much humor as he could muster. The company would send a replacement in the morning.

Police learned the thugs used pistols with silencers to take out lights in the parking lot. That way, no one in the apartments heard anything to alert police. Eric identified the injured man as the same person who struggled with him in the restaurant parking lot.

"Jimmie" will have to hire more heavies if he continues this crazy "kill-Eric" game. How do they find all these murder-for-hire people? Is there a website, Killers, Inc.? Still nothing pointed directly to Overshoot Mining.

Have I lost all worry about danger? There goes my promise to Sarah already! I'd better call her. What can I say? How much can she tolerate? Is it fair to expose her to so much worry that her boyfriend might not be around for their next dinner date? Will I even make it to our first counseling session, let alone live through any period of engagement or, if we ever reach the next stage, marriage? Eric beat himself up with these questions.

I'll try to be calm. "Hi Sarah. Guess what happened?" He explained as best he could and assured her of his safety. Her side of the phone conversation felt strained and subdued. She said little. Eric prayed with Sarah over the phone. It made sense, what with all the violence.

She responded weakly, "I love you." As she was hanging up, Eric heard her begin to cry. That night, sleep didn't come easily for him. *What's happening to our relationship?*

Chapter 14

The next day Eric had another rental. He visited evidence storage at the Pulaski County sheriff's office to inspect Fogel's recordings. Amy led him to a viewing room. "We haven't had time to look at all these. Maybe you can find what you're looking for."

"I hope so. This whole affair's out of control. Too many people getting hurt."

He plunged into the recordings with a fresh enthusiasm to verify that Watson and Sam Beechtree from Overshoot Mining were present. Sam's image was present on a legal listing website, so identification should be easy. Eric also hoped to see evidence of poisoning. Hours passed as he watched videos and listened to voices. It seemed a little eerie to watch and listen to a man he would never meet on the street. The deceased Abe McDonnell ate a meal and argued with the shysters. Eric never met Abe but felt he knew the man from interviews with relatives and by viewing the recordings.

One of the Overshoot employees was the paralegal. Watson appeared in most of the videos. The other man gave his name as Sam Beechtree. So, Watson told the truth. Eric breathed a sigh of relief. *There's no question the crooked lawyer is Beechtree.* Plus, his image matched the official website featuring Sam Beechtree. *Fogel's sketches are worthless. Maybe he was trying to avoid being a direct witness in the case. It doesn't matter now. The recordings are clear who the Overshoot reps were.* Eric looked for any evidence of poisoning during the meals but could find none. Beechtree must have been very sly to avoid incriminating himself on the video. *I only have Watson's testimony to accuse Beechtree as the one who poisoned Abe. Got to keep him safe!*

Beechtree didn't seem to do anything overtly illegal during the meetings. Lots of haggling and arguing disturbed their meals, but no threats. *Did I miss something in the tapes?* He finally decided to call Sean McDonnell. Maybe his attorneys could use some of the tapes as evidence when the case came to court. Eric hoped the judge would allow it. He left the sheriff's station deflated.

Pausing in the parking lot, Eric called Megan and asked her to find out what she could about Sam Beechtree. He drove disheartened back to his office. When he arrived, he found Megan burning up her search engines as she compiled information on Beechtree. Eric knew not to disturb her concentration. He settled in his chair to work on the geology of the area around Abe's farm.

Joseph arrived and told Eric about his escapades sampling farm wells. Miraculously, he visited Abe's house and well without being seen by the guards.

"Joseph," said Eric. "You're stealthy as a cat. What did your magic powers of observation tell you? If something's out there, you must have picked it up."

"While near the mine site, I found a sheet of paper with the guards' schedule of shifts. That might help, if we need to visit the property. It tells when the foreman is on site. You might want to visit soon. It's not easy to see inside the mine from the farmhouse where the well is located."

"I agree. A visit will be necessary."

"The water analyses are on speed dial. You should have them shortly."

As Joseph spoke, e-mails began to arrive with data on some of the wells. Entering data into a GIS map of the area, a pattern emerged. Without surprise, Abe's well fairly bristled with lethal chemicals. *Good thing Sean McDonnell didn't drink from his well. I wonder if pollutants reached the well while Abe was alive. Overshoot's attorneys could argue that Abe's illness was due to bad well water. Grrr.* As Eric suspected, nearby wells showed signs of pollution similar to Abe's well. Overshoot's mine was the logical source.

Sitting in his chair with fingers steepled, Eric mulled over the map. *I've got to have an iron clad case to propose closing the mine.* "Joseph, can you expand your survey of water wells in ever widening circles with the mine at the center?"

"Of course." Joseph grabbed his jacket and boxes of sample bottles. *This will take some time, but the study must be done properly to stand up in court. We must prove the mine as a sole source of contaminants.* A bull's eye of data points around the site could close the mine, but what about the murders and attempted murders? *That requires a different set of data.*

Megan chirped, "Got the home and phone of Sam Beechtree. He's well hidden, I'd say. Must not want anybody to know how to find him. His home is in a high-end neighborhood."

"I'm on it!" Eric ran to his rental to pay Mr. Beechtree an unannounced visit. He grabbed a quick late lunch on the way. Eric mulled over questions to ask Beechtree. The man's residence gave the appearance of an estate. Architecture and surrounding grounds were elaborate. *Must have a ground keeping crew to maintain this place. Serious money.*

He rang the bell and waited. The door opened to reveal Mr. Beechtree dressed in casual attire. *Probably taking a day off from his questionable office work.*

Eric introduced himself and asked if they might talk. Sam invited Eric in and ushered him to a spacious living area. *Matches the elaborate grounds. Beechtree is no ordinary Arkansas lawyer. He's tied into a siphon with a serious cash draw.* Seated, Eric began, "Mr. Beechtree, I've watched hours of video and audio as you badgered Mr. Abe McDonnell into signing a fallacious contract and will, designed to rip off his heirs and line the pockets of Overshoot Mining. I want to know what your company stands to gain by this terrible act. You, as an attorney, could face severe repercussions if these recordings are brought to light."

Beechtree showed signs of being shaken by Eric's abrupt words. He stared wide-eyed at Eric for a long minute. His normally controlled lawyerly voice choked and his words became jerky when he finally managed a feeble response. "I . . . don't quite have an adequate answer for you, Mr. Bonfield. You seem to have the upper hand at this moment."

"Tell me what your corrupt organization is doing on Abe McDonnell's property."

"I'm not privy to everything Overshoot Mining does with their properties."

"That's a bunch of lawyer garbage! You know very well what they do."

Beechtree tried to regain control of his emotions, but Eric's attacks kept coming. "And, I'll go a step further, Mr. Beechtree. The criminals your company hired to murder me are responsible for the deaths of several persons, some of whom are relatives of Mr. McDonnell. And that doesn't include all those thugs who are now in the morgue or hospitalized. And then there are those in jail. You are knee deep in this muck. If your license to practice law in Arkansas isn't in jeopardy, then your name will be mud when the media finish with you. Now, tell me what Overshoot is doing!"

"I . . . I . . . need to see my attorney."

"I'll bet you do! In the meantime, what I've just said about your illegal recording of Mr. McDonnell will soon be public knowledge. Why not avoid huge embarrassment and possible disbarment? I don't know what can be done for you, but it might depend on what you tell me about Overshoot Mining."

Red faced and flustered, Beechtree seemed unable to respond.

"Very well, here's my card. Call my office when you have something to say." And with that, Eric left Mr. Beechtree sitting frustrated in his luxurious living room.

The interview with Sam Beechtree went famously, or at least I hope so. He smiled. *I fed Beechtree just enough information to frighten him into action. Maybe he'll spill the bowl of hidden names and evidence.* Eric felt that Beechtree seemed well suited for the role of a crooked lawyer working for a murderous business, if one could call it a business. *For all I know, Sam might really be "Jimmie", the intermediary who contracts outsiders to kill opponents. At this moment, Sam might be pinpointing me for extermination by the firm's next goon.* He shuddered and thought of Sarah.

Eric drove out of Sam Beechtree's magnificent neighborhood. He realized how tired he felt. He was chasing and being chased. This thought stirred a new line of concern. *What kind of career life do I really want to live?*

For the first time since taking up detective work, Eric mentally scratched his head and asked a life-molding question out loud, "What do I want from my career?" This query smoldered on the way to his office. By the time he parked and turned off the engine, Eric shook the thought from his mind and refocused on the problem at hand. *Maybe I'll take up deep questions with Sarah later.*

Eric flopped into his office chair. It creaked. Not knowing where to go from here, Eric's mind slid to the annoying chair he used every day. "Megan, can you order a new chair . . ." was all he got out when the office phone rang.

"Yes, I will . . . and it's Sean McDonnell. He wants to know the latest details."

"Tell him I'll be there in 15 minutes." Eric didn't trust the office phone with sensitive information. "Have him come to Harry's Café, so we can talk in private."

As Eric dashed for the door, Megan yelled that McDonnell would be there. Harry's Café was half-way between Eric's office and the McDonnell bank building. Knowing how efficient his client could be, Eric wanted to reach the restaurant before Mr. McDonnell.

Sean McDonnell is a likeable man in many ways. A strictly honest person who earns his money the old-fashioned way, McDonnell believes in hard work. No one ever accused him of dealing under the table. Not that Sean exudes pleasantries. He expects adherence to high ethical principles, and anyone who doesn't follow those ideals ends up on his bad list. *My own ideals match Sean's belief system; we rarely have conflicts over principles. Our personalities are, however, quite different.*

Eric skidded into the café's parking lot just as McDonnell's ancient pickup lumbered into a parking space. A meeting with Mr.

McDonnell never took much time; they were anything but long and windy conversations. The session would be short and to the point. *I like that. No use wasting time on chit-chat when lots of unanswered questions swirl through the air; plus, the court date is creeping up.*

The café was small but quiet and out of range from prying eyes. Eric, the meticulous note-taker, kept his notebook at the ready so he didn't miss any details to relay to McDonnell. After Eric exhausted all he had uncovered to date and stared blankly at the ceiling, McDonnell said, "I don't think we have enough for an open and shut case, do you?"

"No sir, I agree there're still too many loose ends, and none connect directly with Overshoot Mining just yet; especially weak is a clear relationship to the murders."

"Eric, I really want to know what they're up to at the mine on Abe's farm. Can you find out?"

Eric squirmed in his seat. Invasion of the land didn't set well with him. But he knew that might be the only way to answer Sean's question. "I'll give it a try, Mr. McDonnell."

"Good, good! Let me know when you have information . . . any information at all."

"Sure thing. I'll let you know." *What'm I getting into now? Am I in over my head?* When their session ended, Eric called Sarah. He needed fresh inspiration. She always inspired him; either that or she got his mind off things that bothered him.

"I'm at the office right now, so let's have a working dinner. I'm anxious to know what you've found out." She sounded much better than their last phone talk.

Eric drove to his apartment for a quick nap. Weariness was catching up. Conversations with Sean McDonnell quickly drained him.

The drive to Sarah's farm countered the anxiety of someone shooting at him, or racing to rescue Sarah from kidnappers, or a long list of other events he'd rather not deal with right now. She lived far enough out in the country to be away from most negative effects of the city, except for invaders into her home, shootouts, and *. . . I guess it's exciting out here after all!*

Is Sarah my girlfriend or fiancé? Since I've yet to kneel with a small rock on a gold band in my hand, I'd better stick to serious girlfriend.

When he arrived at her farm, Sarah seemed to have recovered from her phone conversations with Eric. They chatted all the way to the restaurant. Eric enjoyed hearing Sarah's voice. Her alto rose and fell with an enchanting rhythm. She had clear diction, and her thoughts were right on. *What a pleasure to be with her!* At the restaurant, Eric wistfully looked into Sarah's eyes and said, "Where did you get those beautiful eyes?"

"Oh, I found them while looking into yours."

Sarah changed the subject and asked about the events of his day. "I nailed the crooked lawyer and expect to hear from him shortly. At least I hope to. Of course, there are other possibilities." He saw Sarah glance at him with a frown and knew she was thinking about what negative events might happen.

"Sean McDonnell's chomping at the bit to find out what those Overshoot people are doing on his land. It's up to me to guess how to discover what's going on. The court date's coming up, and McDonnell doesn't want to enter that event flat-footed. And then there're those people who're witnesses in this case. I've got to keep them under wraps, if that's possible. This band of cutthroats will stop at nothing to get their way. Murder, Inc., would make a good website name for this so-called mining company."

Their food came, and Eric asked Sarah to say a blessing. She spoke heartfelt thanks for Eric's safety and prayed this awful case would come to a lawful close with bad folk behind bars and the killing stopped. Eric offered an "Amen".

After finishing their salads, Sarah asked, "How can you can find out what's happening on the mine site? You've already said there're no public records to go on. Why don't you brainstorm for a few minutes? I'll take notes." She reached for a pen and notepad in her purse. Sarah knew Eric was a verbal thinker.

"Great idea," he said. Then began an hour-long excursion to Eric's quarry of thoughts.

Sarah nodded and smiled as she said, "You're an excellent verbal processor." Then she started to ask questions to help Eric prioritize his options.

What a keen mind! She'd make a nice partner for our firm. Wait a minute; is she a compatriot in business or a potential lover? Can she be both? Should I marry my business partner? And what about people like Joseph and Megan who're so integral to the firm? Would I let Sarah's ideas trump theirs?

"What're you thinking?"

Embarrassed, Eric said, "I was realizing how much you mean to me, and how much you help me with my work."

She blushed and reached for his hand. "The feeling is the same on this side of our table. But let me assure you that I'm happy with my job as a legal secretary and have no intention of working in your office!"

She read my mind! She knew exactly what he was thinking! *How scary is that?*

As usual, the empty restaurant began to echo Sarah and Eric's voices. They looked around and felt self-conscious that all the other customers had left. Their server stood nearby fidgeting, ready to close shop. Eric apologized and gave him a large tip as they hurriedly left and escaped to the humid air outside. At her farm home, they lingered on her porch.

Although their time together focused on a criminal case, intimacy between Sarah and Eric deepened. The topic they discussed didn't seem to matter.

"What do you know about our upcoming session with a counselor? I'm just a little uncertain about what happens."

Sarah smiled. *He's worried about this.* "You've nothing to be concerned about. Her name is Elaine. She has twenty years of experience working with couples. I'm impressed with her degrees, but more than that, I really like her manner. She exudes great wisdom. I like she's a believer; but she practices her faith in such a winsome way that her professionalism isn't negated by her beliefs. She'll work us through lots of topics."

"Will we pass?"

With a laugh, Sarah said, "This isn't a pass-fail course. Sessions focus on how to use our strong areas to build a positive relationship."

"I'm anxious to start!" he said. Eric experienced the deep longing for intimacy present in humans. His life to this point focused on preparing for work and working at what he loved to do. *Now I want to see what the rest of life might be like with a family.* He had no illusions of an idyllic life. *I see my role as a godly husband and father who assists my family to not just survive but thrive.*

"Eric, what're you thinking about?" Sarah broke his musing.

"Just wondering where life is taking us."

"I hope it's taking us together." As she spoke, Sarah reached for his neck and placed the most passionate kiss on his lips Eric could imagine.

Eric tickled her, they both laughed, and he almost fell off the porch. He chuckled as he staggered toward his car. He waved at the beautiful person who stood laughing at her doorstep. She was almost bent over with her gasps. As he pulled away from her driveway, Eric said out loud, "She's some woman." He caught himself, shook his head, and momentarily returned to high and lofty thoughts; then he paused for a chuckle.

Chapter 15

The next morning Eric got an early call from Megan. *Calling this early has gotta mean something's up.*

"It's from a Mr. Beechtree. Says he wants to talk with you. Says to meet him at the restaurant you and he know about for a late breakfast."

Eric's heart sped up a notch. *Why there? That's where so much mayhem took place. Was this a trap? Or maybe it's to keep away from the Overshoot group's prying eyes so he can come clean.* Either way, Eric decided to take no chances. He called the Hot Springs County sheriff's office and asked for support, just in case trouble reared its head. No problem. Someone would have his back. *Whew! I don't want Sarah to get the ultimate phone call!*

After the death of the owner, the Fogel family reopened the restaurant following his funeral. It seemed strange to be meeting possible murderers where their crimes were committed. *But that's Beechtree's choice. What else can I do?*

He drove toward the rendezvous with mixed feelings. Normally, Eric enjoyed the scenic drive, but not today. *Would this crooked lawyer spill the dirt on his bosses, or might a thug wait to waylay me before I even have breakfast? Lots of possibilities.* He didn't have long to wait; the restaurant lay just ahead. Eric cautiously drove toward the parking lot. He glanced to his right, then left, in his rear-view mirror, and to the front. *No suspicious activity.*

The lot held a few pickups and a couple cars. *Just some late breakfast patrons, I suppose.* Two cars caught his attention: a BMW and a Porsche. *Serious money. Must be Overshoot cars.* Owners of upscale vehicles didn't often eat at Fogel's restaurant. The Overshoot vehicles stood out amidst the Ford and Chevy pickups. A good way to start a fight in the Highlands would be to argue about pickup brands.

Eric parked his rented vehicle between the expensive cars. Any bomber who wanted to demolish his car, and him in it, would also take out both Overshoot cars. Such a precaution might prove useful. Eric exited his car and walked up the steps. Still no rifle shots. *Might not be a trap after all.* On entering the restaurant, he saw Sam Beechtree seated in a booth with a well-dressed gentleman. Eric walked over and greeted Beechtree.

"Eric, I want you to meet Mr. Franklin, the CEO of Overshoot Mining, Inc."

Without looking too shocked, Eric composed himself and shook hands. Franklin's handshake was firm and bespoke of physical strength. "I'm glad to meet you. And to what do I owe the opportunity of meeting with you and Mr. Beechtree?"

"Eric, my attorney here says you've spoken with him about some rather serious matters. I thought I'd come and clear up any questions you might have."

"I'm all ears, so to speak."

"Just what would you like to know, Mr. Bonfield?"

"Let's start with the illegal videoing of interviews with Mr. Abe McDonnell. I've watched this blatant method of trying to badger Abe into signing those ridiculous will and contract documents. I've got evidence that Abe received poison to bring him into submission, and that an Overshoot representative, Mr. Beechtree here, practically signed the documents for him. Now I want to know exactly what you're doing with the McDonnell property. I'll pursue the attempts on my life and the murders of McDonnell relatives shortly."

Franklin appeared to be unaware of the poisoning accusation, or how the documents were signed, or at least he put on a good show. He glared at Beechtree, who shrugged his shoulders nervously. Franklin was silent for a minute, then he spoke cautiously. "I can't comment on most of what you are saying, Mr. Bonfield. You'll have to deal with my other attorneys who don't happen to be here right now. About all I can say is that we're a legitimate company dealing with various forms of mineral resource development. Our work on the McDonnell property is proprietary and not available for public knowledge just yet. I don't have any more to say."

"Very well, then perhaps you'd like to comment about attempts on my life and the murders of several people who knew of your fallacious activities. This mayhem had sent many people to their graves, the hospital, or jail. What is your part in this?"

"I don't have anything to say," Franklin managed. "My attorneys are necessary for any further discussions to take place."

"Then I guess our discussion is over," said Eric. He shrugged, turned, and walked out of the restaurant without even ordering breakfast. Beechtree and Franklin sat staring after Eric. They were digesting the bombshell dropped in their laps instead of bacon and eggs.

Eric drove out of the lot as he carefully looked in all directions. He saw nothing, except a sheriff deputy's car carefully hidden by the trees. Eric waved at the officer. She waved back. *Nice that she's here.*

On the way back to town, Eric considered the verbal grenade he tossed to the Overshoot CEO and his rotten lawyer. Eric liked to use his information at the right time to generate the most shock. Sometimes it worked, and sometimes there were unforeseen consequences. Since Eric didn't tell them what evidence he had, they didn't know if this included living persons, or written documents, or something else. *I hope this strategy gives me a measure of safety. If the evidence is only with me, then murdering me makes sense. If evidence exists outside of my person, I should be safe. Hope this will help Sarah feel more at ease.*

He smiled and thought how the CEO and attorney must be chewing on what he said. *What'll be their next move? Maybe they'll just sit on their hands and do nothing. That approach could be their safest choice.* Then the ball would be in Sean McDonnell and Eric's court. Sean and Eric must then produce the evidence and convince a court of the illegal nature of the will and contract. *There might be other scenarios. I doubt the two men I left glaring at me will decide on their own what to do. Will they have a board meeting? I'll see what Sean would like for us to do. He's a creative person.*

At McDonnell's office, Eric described his confrontation with the top dog at Overshoot Mining and his sleazy lawyer. Sean smiled at Eric's brash approach. "I like to let them have it without warning. I try to judge their reactions and how my comments affect their story. It often works. I have some ideas about how to proceed, but they depend on how the gang responds." Eric outlined a plan he was thinking about. Sean endorsed it enthusiastically. Eric liked Sean. He was a man of action who valued and rewarded good ideas.

Sean and Eric agreed to wait a couple days. Perhaps time might flush the bad guys out from their cover. Depending on their response, Sean and Eric could move forward with their plan. Sean McDonnell didn't like to wait, but he knew the ball sat in the Overshoot's court. Eric left Sean's office smiling. He enjoyed talking with Sean. He usually left these sessions inspired and ready for action, although the meetings were tiring.

Eric walked around his car out of habit as much as anything. *No evidence of danger.* He started to open the door but thought better of it. Instead, he walked to the edge of the building to use the structure as a shield. He pushed the remote start button. A horrific explosion shattered the vehicle. Debris shot past Eric's hiding place as he drew back just in time to avoid being decapitated.

Shaking his head, Eric realized the Overshoot clan decided not to waste time trying to silence their nemesis. Eric called police and the car rental company. *Surely the rental folk will run out of patience. They've lost too many cars.* But Eric's insurance always paid for damages. *Maybe my agent gets some publicity out of this.* Violent events made local news, and the insurance and rental companies names always appeared in the stories.

Eric started to phone Sean McDonnell's office, but Sean heard the explosion and was running down the stairs to see what happened.

McDonnell rushed outside and started to ask Eric about the explosion when a bullet grazed Sean's arm. He stumbled away. "Get back inside!" Eric shouted. McDonnell ran to the door as additional bullets knocked bits of concrete from the side of the building. Eric ducked around the corner of the structure again as the sniper shifted fire from McDonnell to Eric. Dust and concrete fragments filled the air as bullets pinged off Eric's hiding spot. Eric shouted into his cell phone, "Shooter! Come fast." *The explosion was a decoy to draw Sean out of the bank.*

Police cars raced to the area. The gunman riddled Eric's hiding spot. Eric tried to judge the location of the sniper from the angles made by debris kicked up by the bullets. He alerted police where to look. Police officers crowded around the area. Eric screamed into his phone, "I think it's that same empty building used by the other sniper. Get in back and seal off the tunnel entrance!"

Officers fanned out and charged into the building from all directions. Shooting stopped momentarily. Eric's suspicion about the tunnel proved correct. He heard muffled shots. *Different sounds. Police pistols mixed with rifle shots.* After a few minutes, quiet resumed, and an officer called Eric.

"Had a shootout with this guy. One officer down with a leg wound, and another nursing a grazed cheek. Sniper didn't do as well. He's headed to the hospital. Wounds look life-threatening."

Eric went to the door of Sean's building, brushed concrete dust from the handle, and stepped inside. Sean McDonnell waited a few paces from the door. He was hiding behind a pillar. "Did they get him?"

"Yeah. He wounded a couple of officers, but they shot him. He's on his way to the ER. Are you hurt?"

"Just a scratch. I'll get it cleaned, bandaged, and be good as new."

Eric stood in amazement as he stared at Sean McDonnell. Sean was a tough businessman who didn't seem fazed by this attempt on his life. "Well, what do we do now?" Sean asked.

"Let's put our plan into action right away."

Sean paused and said, "I don't mind the danger. But I didn't hire you to face violence."

Eric laughed nervously. "I think danger is part of anything I do. What's a little more?"

Sean nodded. "We're both in somebody's line of fire, so why wait? Let's get this thing going! Get a good night's rest." He rolled up his sleeve and examined the wound. He shrugged and walked upstairs for first aid.

Eric watched the banker climb the stairs two at a time. *This guy must have been some athlete in his day!*

Representatives of Eric's car rental company eventually arrived. "Mr. Bonfield, you set the record for vehicles destroyed by one person renting from us. How do you do it?" She smiled as she handed Eric the keys. "Oh, and yes, it does have remote starting capability."

"Not my plan, but I do seem to be in the car demolishing business." All of them laughed. "This one looks like it just escaped the crusher at the recycling center. You guys are onto me for sure."

"You'll never guess how hard it is to keep up with the special fleet of just the right cars for you!" The reps laughed as they drove away.

Chapter 16

That evening Eric picked up Sarah at her farm. She waited anxiously. *I never know what car he'll show up driving.*

When he pulled onto her driveway, she walked quickly to his car and got in before he could open his door. *Sarah must be on edge. She always waits for me at her door.* The redness in her eyes told the tale. Eric started to apologize, but she stopped him before three words exited his mouth.

"It's not your fault somebody tried to blow you up and then shoot you down." Her tense face gave way to tears welling up and running down her cheeks. "I . . . I . . . I don't know how to handle all this!" Sarah's hands covered her face and she sobbed. Her breath came in gasps and her words inaudible.

What do I say? No clue. All his creative thoughts and explanations in prior conversations seemed trite. The woman he loved cried convulsively over him. Their relationship seemed so fragile at this moment.

Reaching across the seat, he took her in his arms and said nothing. Eventually Sarah's sobs subsided. *Should I say something? Probably not.*

Finally, she turned her face up to his and said, "Eric, I love you. I don't want anything to happen to you. Do you understand?"

"You're right to be concerned for me. I get into awful scrapes. I want this whole terrible thing to go away; I really do. I wish I could just walk away."

"I don't want you to walk away. I just don't know how to deal with all this . . . this not knowing . . . not knowing if I'll see you in one piece or not!"

At last he felt he could gently release her as she relaxed her grip on him. "I hope our counselor can give us perspective on all this."

She brushed her hair back and cleared her throat. "That'll be late Monday afternoon."

"Sounds good." He felt worn out from all the tension. *Whew! That was intense.*

He lightly kissed her upturned and sweaty forehead. She closed her eyes and stretched her lips toward his. Eric tilted his head toward hers and their faces seemed as one. Eric said, "Dinner sounds really good to me. How about you? Where would you like to go?"

"I don't care, but I feel so rumpled. I've got to change and fix my hair."

He quickly jumped out of the car and opened the door for her.

Sarah reappeared in a fresh blue dress that hugged her in all the right places. With the effects of tears muted, her pretty face almost wore a smile. *How does she do this?* Eric escorted her to his car and opened the door. The hinges groaned as if they were exhausted. He seated her comfortably before closing the door with a rattle. His father raised him to pay special attention to old fashioned etiquette when taking a lady out. Sarah recognized this choreographed detail and thanked him. She could hardly be called a woman steeped in ancient southern tradition. Yet she allowed herself the pleasure of her gentleman's attention. She made eyes at Eric, and he almost blushed. How those eyes spoke volumes!

For reasons unclear, Eric thought about Sarah's background. Although her farm sat on the Coastal Plain, she displayed little of the drawl that most southern residents of Arkansas spoke. *Probably like me. She and I are affected by the city and the atmosphere of college. I could drawl with the best of them, but no need. I work with a wide variety of clients from the Southern Midlands Ozark dialect to deep south folk. I love them all. Most are good people.*

Conversation stayed away from the mining case. They talked of her fascination with the out-of-doors. She wanted to travel, but her parents were tied to their farm. The open road sounded so good to her.

On the other hand, Eric traveled quite a bit. His geological training led him to many states. He especially enjoyed geology field camp in Colorado. Measuring rock layers in the foothills and mapping features in the mountains heightened his love for the planet. His work in the oil patch restricted him mainly to Texas. When he decided to be an independent consultant, he returned to his home state. Work led him all over Arkansas and adjoining states. His interest in solving crime cases grew out of his love for solving complex geological problems.

They ordered their usual fare at Antonio's, relaxed, and said little until their food arrived. Finally, Sarah turned their attention to more serious matters.

"Eric?"

"Yes?"

"I want you to know something about me that directly affects you and our relationship."

Eric's eyes widened, and perspiration beads started to form on his forehead. *Oh no! Is she going to break up with me?*

"I want you to know, I love you. That's a fact. And all this talk about me being concerned for your safety is my emotions expressing themselves. It's got nothing to do with my love for you. I want to be with you through thick and thin, or as the vows say, 'for better or worse'." She blushed, "Oops, I guess that sounds like a marriage proposal, doesn't it? I don't want to steal your traditional responsibilities. I believe in the work you do; it's important, and I support you."

Eric let out a deep breath he'd been holding and felt his muscles relax. "That's the most beautiful speech I've ever heard. Can you say it again?"

She gave him a love poke on his wounded shoulder, which caused him to winch.

Now it's my turn. After a few moments of silence, he laid down his fork. "I want you to know something too. Never have I felt love for a woman before I met you. I've always heard people talk about what love is supposed to be like. But now that I know you, I agree with all I've heard; love is a wondrous experience. And you're the object of all my love. I want to commit that love to you forever."

They sat across the table, their food growing cold. Sarah realized they both almost proposed to each other. As wait staff began to shutter the restaurant, Eric suggested they should go.

Their doorstep ritual included an embrace that generated pain signals from several of Eric's battle wounds. *But it's worth every moment.*

Chapter 17

The following morning, Eric took his time getting ready. He ambled over to get his bandage fix from Alice.

"You're healing very nicely. You can forget these bandages soon, in my opinion."

"All the result of your skilled care. I can't thank you enough." He handed her a gift card.

"You didn't need to do that!"

"But I did anyway." He laughed.

She laughed and sent him back to his apartment. *Got to wait for Sean McDonnell's call.* Eric alerted the Malvern sheriff about the possible need for backup. "We're going into the tiger's lair. Don't know how things will go."

"No worries. Ah'll have ma best deputies standin' by. We want these murders stopped."

"Me too. Thanks."

"We want ta get back ta writin' speedin' tickets and eatin' doughnuts." They both laughed.

Sean called. "I'm ready. How about you?"

"Let's do this! The sheriff has our backs."

Eric followed Sean at a distance to avoid the appearance of forming a convoy. *No evidence of a tail.* Sean drove west into the country toward Abe McDonnell's farm.

As Sean approached the land Abe had bequeathed to him, Eric stopped and waited, hidden from the view of Overshoot's guards. Eric listened to the hidden mic Sean carried. He heard the initial sound of Sean's pickup stopping by the mine entrance. Sean greeted one of the guards and asked to come onto the property. The guard called a number and relayed the request. After a few minutes of waiting, the guard said Sean could enter.

Eric heard the pickup move forward for a few minutes. The engine stopped. Sean spoke into the mic, "I can see the quarry or mine or whatever it is."

An employee came to the pickup and said he would be Sean's guide. Eric heard the crunch of boots on rough ground. "So, what do you do here?" asked Sean. The man mumbled something and pointed out a large earthmoving machine. Several sat idle.

"Are you guys mining something here?" Another incoherent response met Sean's direct question. Conversation was very limited.

Eric heard the rumble of a large truck as it entered the open pit. The driver turned off his engine and waited. "What's he hauling?" Sean wanted to know.

"Not a full load," was all his guide would offer. Clearly this employee was keeping Sean away from anything that might reveal what Overshoot did at the mine.

After an hour, Sean thanked the guide and drove out of the mining area. Eric followed Sean to a rural café where they ate a very late breakfast. "What'd you see?" Eric asked.

"Not much. There're obvious pieces of equipment used to push dirt and rocks around. The truck must haul something. You could tell by the way it drove; it was full of something heavy. I've been around surface mines before and this one is strange. I saw no hints of any useful commodity being excavated. Very puzzling."

Eric thought so too. He pulled a box of specimens from his back seat. He wanted to see if Sean could recognize any ore that might be present. Sean inspected the samples, but none clicked with him. "I didn't see anything like what you've got here; all I saw were a few pieces of magnetite and tan colored rocks."

"Wonder what they're doing?" asked Eric.

"Wish I knew."

"Did you see any colored minerals?"

"No, not a one. Just ordinary reddish-brown rocks. A little magnetite is scattered around, but there's hardly enough to mention. Might even have been brought in from someplace else."

"At least this confirms what we've heard from other people who visited the site."

Then Sean said, "There might be other rocks there, but the guide carefully led me only to certain areas. I don't think I saw more than ten percent of the dug-up site."

"State records don't say what's happening at the mine. Reports from Overshoot Mining are gibberish; they're legal chatter about prospects and such. I'm afraid we've reached an impasse in finding what goes on at the mine." Sean's inspection yielded no new thoughts. *What goes on when we aren't there?*

They decided to let the mine problem rest for a day. The court date wasn't so imminent that they'd have to rush ahead half-baked. "Maybe we should wait for the Overshoots' next move." Sean shook his head. "I don't like to wait, but guess we've got no choice."

Then Eric's eyes brightened. "Satellite photography! Why didn't I think of it before?"

"What're you talking about?"

"I'd thought about using a drone to photograph the mine site but knew this bordered on illegality. Besides, guards would probably shoot down anything that looked suspicious. The government regularly takes high altitude photos of the area and these are available to the general public. What better way to see what's happened over time at the mine?"

Sean shrugged his shoulders. "Might be worth a try."

They left the café, and Eric rushed to his office. He asked Megan to search for as many aerial photographs and satellite images of Abe's farm as she could find.

"Will do." Her internet skills kicked into high gear.

It was Friday and Megan normally didn't work Saturday, but she caught Eric's excitement and didn't mind hunkering over her computer the next day. *If he needs it, I'll get it!* Her husband was on another convention tour, and the married kids lived several states away. *What'll I do on a dull Saturday anyway? Besides, a punched clock yields time-and-a-half coin.*

When Saturday came, Eric beat her to the office. Megan was shocked! *He must really be onto something!* She knew Eric's mind was drilling a hole into a problem. She smiled as he gazed at his computer screen. She seated herself and her own fingers drummed out requests for any images of Abe's farm. After two hours Megan ran into roadblocks on the information highway. She called over her shoulder, "You'll need to wait until Monday to download satellite data. I got some aerial photo stuff for you, but the system on satellites is down."

"Thanks for working on this." He sighed. "No use pushing when the government isn't functional!"

Megan shut down her computer and Eric walked her to her car. As they walked down the steps to the parking lot, Eric said, "Tomorrow is Sunday and I need some serious spiritual renewal. On Monday Sarah and I've got our first session with the counselor." Megan smiled knowingly and waved goodbye. She couldn't wait to text her husband this latest news.

Eric returned to his office computer to see what Megan discovered. *I hope Monday shines new light on the case. Satellite imagery and aerial photography might hold the key to what's really happening at the mine.* For the moment, Eric had to be satisfied with at least the prospect of a breakthrough. He inspected aerial photography Megan had located. After working through the images, Eric screwed up his face. *Not enough to tell me what I need to know.*

He shifted his focus to the weekend. *What a great time to relax and get some relief from all the pressure. Stress makes me tired.* After putting the finishing touches on a geological consulting project, he closed shop for the rest of the weekend. Late afternoon shadows were sneaking across the parking lot. Eric tiptoed out the back door and closed it gently, just in case someone was watching his office. He pressed the remote start and his car started without exploding. *Now that's something different!* He headed to his apartment, sleep on his mind.

Sunday was cloudy but without rain. Eric fixed a leisurely breakfast, balanced for once, and drove to pick up Sarah for church. His eyes flew open when she stepped through her farmhouse doorway in a bright green and white dress complete with matching white shoes. He felt a tingle in his chest when she walked briskly toward him. Sarah in any apparel turned on his attraction magnet. But his childhood upbringing favored church attendance in classic attire. *After all, this is the north end of the South!*

Eric opened the car door for Sarah at the church parking lot. She took his arm and her heels clicked on the concrete as they walked. "How difficult is it to walk in high heels?"

She laughed and said, "It just takes practice."

Eric's pastor stood smiling at the church door. His robe bore evidence of summer's humidity as perspiration dripped from Pastor Erickson's chin. Eric knew this man of the cloth stood outside to greet his parishioners regardless of weather. He hugged Sarah and grabbed Eric's hand with power. Eric wondered what Reverend Erickson did before he became a preacher. That handshake spoke volumes.

As they entered the stain-glass windowed sanctuary, Eric looked at the buzzing crowd. This was a well-loved congregation. Eric saw many colors and ethnicities sprinkled around the room like candies on Christmas cookies. *I love the atmosphere here every Sunday.* "God's love is for everybody" read a sign outside the sanctuary. *I agree. And that extends to criminals I try to catch.* He smiled and followed Sarah who trailed behind an usher. As they brushed legs of others in the row where the usher led them, Eric nodded to people he passed and shook an occasional hand.

Opposite ends of the social spectrum sat side-by-side. Prominent business execs and simple people of the Highlands were equals here. Eric reached across the pew to shake hands with a five-year-old boy and his grandfather. Some came from long lines of aristocrats dating back to pre-Civil War times. Others came from a background of slavery. Their families traced times back to progenitors who took a forced ship ride from Africa. Now they occupied seats next to relatives of deceased slave owners. What a contrast! Only God and people who care can bring this about!

The choir and music opened with a traditional hymn but quickly jumped into a contemporary worship sequence. The pastor's sermon came from Jesus' story about the Good Samaritan. In addition to providing cultural background to understand what the story meant to Jesus' hearers, the minister wove the narrative into today's problems. Contrasts between cultures and how to deal with them from a Christian perspective climaxed the homily.

Eric applied the pastor's words. His small office consisted of a middle-class female office manager and a partner born in Mexico who immigrated to the United States as a young adult. Eric's clients stretched from struggling entrepreneurs who eked out a living just above poverty level to big businesses needing help to solve a short-term problem.

At lunch, Sarah recounted her own experiences growing up on a farm. Their community consisted of families with distant relatives who bore the stripes of slaves and weariness of sharecroppers. Her parents were wonderful people but, for reasons she never understood, didn't have much social contact with these neighbors. Personally, Sarah played with all the neighborhood children. As an adult, Sarah easily made friends with immigrants of Asian background.

That evening they shared a light supper at a casual restaurant. They returned to Sarah's home for coffee and a movie on TV to conclude their day.

He slept well that night. After a morning shower and shave, Eric went through the ritual of inspecting his car. His video capture system failed after the first night. He had quipped to Megan last week that a good day began without a bang.

Breakfast at one of the quaint hole-in-the-wall cafes in downtown Little Rock attracted Eric. He disliked fast food even though that was standard fare too many times. *Fred's Spot* offered everything *but* quick service. Eric waited for a space at one of the half-dozen tables that always seemed occupied in the early morning hours. Fred waited on tables, took your money, and swapped gossip, while his wife Emily stirred pancake batter and flipped eggs. The extra minutes offered by eating at Fred's provided a calm before the day's storm.

Megan's discoveries waited for him as he entered the office. If Eric was clear about what data he needed, she didn't disappoint. Lots of digital images eagerly awaited previewing. Eric's instructions were specific: all aerial and satellite surveys of the Overshoot mining site from a month before the suspicious company occupied the site right up to the present.

With software, Eric adjusted all images to the same size. This allowed him to overlay the pictures one after the other, to detect any variations in position or size of objects, as well as see new features. This formed a crude video that reminded Eric of the old Keystone Cops flickering movies. The pre-Overshoot images permitted Eric to become familiar with the landscape. He identified buildings, trees, roads, fences, and vehicles. Eric watched with fascination as the mining company moved equipment on site and began to push soil and rock around. From prior experience, Eric could identify most of the mining equipment.

It became obvious nothing was removed from the mine. All earth materials were simply pushed to new locations on site. Then, Eric noticed trucks entering. They arrived, apparently full, and left empty. Imagination was needed to fill in blank spaces between image shots. Eric never saw any earthen materials leave the site. The traffic reminded him of a landfill, not a mine. He plotted changes in texture and color of material being dumped to see where it ended up. Only one small part of the so-called mine received the foreign deposits. Over 90% of the cleared area showed no signs of receiving any outside material. Earth from the unused area apparently provided cover for the dumped matter. *Must be to avoid detection.*

Eric said to Megan, "It's time to track those trucks and see where they come from. I've got an idea but need hard proof. Too bad the images aren't frequent enough to follow the trucks. I need on-the-ground information."

Joseph came into the office from collecting well contamination data. "I've got a bunch of well samples to the chem lab for analysis. Should be available soon. How's the Overshoot project coming from your side?"

"We need to change tactics. There's no doubt something is being transported to the site. McDonnell's property is basically a dump. We need to track some of the trucks bringing stuff on site."

"We?"

"Yeah, suppose we split up and follow different trucks. Then we gather info and find out what's going on. How does that sound?"

Joseph smiled and said, "Ah, so that's the plan! I like it. You know, I've always admired the abilities of blood hounds. We're going to do that. Correct?"

"Yep."

"When do we start?"

"From satellite data, I think delivery begins before 9 a.m. If we're there by 8:30, we can tail the trucks after they dump their loads. I suspect the same trucks work all day, so we should be able to locate where they pick up material."

"That way we can pinpoint the type of material being dumped and see if it matches the analyses of water I've collected."

"Exactly! And after we've got clear photo evidence of pickup and delivery, we can squeeze offending companies for details. These are maps of the site and possible stake-out locations for us to set up shop. Concealment is critical, so we can follow trucks without being seen." Eric looked at his watch and remembered his and Sarah's appointment with their counselor was only a half hour away. "Got to go!" And he rushed out the door.

"What's he in such a hurry for," asked Joseph.

"Got a hot date with Sarah and Elaine!" She laughed.

"Sounds different!"

"Keep an eye on Eric. He and Sarah are moving toward something big."

"Got it!" They both laughed.

Chapter 18

Sarah came from work, as did Eric. They converged at the counselor's office; Sarah arrived ahead of Eric who, as usual, came in a rush. "We're a few minutes early, so let's sit in the waiting room to collect our thoughts."

Sarah always knows what to do!

Shortly, Elaine appeared at the door to her office. She had short brown hair and wore a kind smile. *Looks like she's in her forties.* She possessed a welcoming face and invited them into a room with a comfortable chair and sofa. Eric and Sarah shared the sofa.

Elaine began, "Tell me a little about yourselves and why you're here today."

Sarah took the lead and gave some of her background. She told about her family, education, and work. Elaine asked how she and Eric met. Sarah grinned and shared the unusual circumstances of their meeting. She described their almost immediate chemistry.

Then Sarah became sober and told of their mutual concern about whether the danger surrounding their relationship might bias their feelings toward each other.

When Sarah paused to breathe, Elaine turned to Eric and asked him to describe his side of the story. Eric took up the discussion by telling Elaine his background. He echoed Sarah's statements about their relationship.

"What do you hope to gain from our visits?"

Eric said, "I want clarity about our relationship, and if we should move forward."

Sarah agreed enthusiastically.

Elaine said, "I understand the unusual circumstances of your meeting suggest further exploration might be needed before you become too serious. I ask pre-married couples to take an evaluative tool to help pinpoint similarities and differences in personalities, preferences, backgrounds, and a host of other topics. It can be done online. At our next meeting, I'll begin the interpretation."

After the session, they grabbed a quick meal and separated to take the evaluation.

Tuesday dawned with clear skies and no precipitation in sight. *Perfect for capturing criminal activity on video!* Eric ate breakfast in his apartment and mentally prepared himself for tailing a suspect. Bloodhounding came easy to Eric, and he avoided detection by most people. Early morning traffic jams going through Little Rock could be a hassle, so he allowed plenty of time to reach the farm. The city was experiencing unprecedented growth, and road construction never seemed to end. Eric shook his head as he waited at a road repair site. *Growth is okay, but I'm concerned that the crime rate is so high. It's much worse than when I was growing up.* Then he smiled grimly. *I guess that means my P.I. business won't be going down any time soon!*

He drove to the spot by Overshoot's mine which he preselected from satellite photography and called Joseph. His partner sat in a similar position with field glasses, ready to pick up any suspicious truck. *I never get ahead of Megan or Joseph!*

Eric checked the charge on his cell phone and camera. His powerful zoom lens could count nose hairs at 100 yards; it was great for court cases. He and Joseph waited for activity to begin at the mine site. Bees buzzed around Eric's vehicle, attracted by heat from the engine. *Waiting can be boring. This is sort of like a stakeout.* After an hour, a truck appeared and slowly entered the site. *Must be carrying a full load, given the way the vehicle sways from side to side.* Thirty minutes later, the same truck bounced out onto the road, obviously lighter than when it arrived.

"This one's mine!" Joseph said. He began his tail.

A half hour passed before the next truck arrived. *Same song as before. I wonder how much stuff they're dumping here.* When it returned to the road, Eric began his pursuit.

"How's yours coming?" Eric asked Joseph on his cellphone.

"So far, so good. I'm keeping my GPS data log active."

"Excellent. Same here."

GPS data was continually fed into their GIS software. They wanted no mistakes in tracking. After an hour, Joseph reported his truck entered a large chemical complex.

"I'm in a stakeout position. It's not ideal. The site is visible, but I can't quite see what the truck's doing."

Eric's truck entered another plant; this one manufactured fertilizer. Fortunately, Eric's position allowed him to watch the truck pull up to a large storage tank. Video footage recorded the truck as it was filled with material from the tank. *Bingo! Now if the truck will only go back to the same dump and unload. What great data to give state authorities and Sean McDonnell's attorneys!*

Joseph followed his now loaded truck back to the farm. Eric's truck came close on their heels. Eric and Joseph wanted to get to viewing locations where they could record the trucks unloading. Satellite images revealed the best places. Sure enough, they could just see both trucks being unloaded into a deep pit on the site. *Beautiful! Now to spring the trap and find out what these trucks are transporting.*

Eric drove straight to the fertilizer plant and asked to see the manager. He flashed his identification which granted him entry to the office.

"Yes?" said the no-nonsense manager with a fresh crewcut, as Eric walked into a well-appointed suite.

"I'm a private investigator and have evidence that a truck picked up a load at your facility and dumped it illegally on a farm not far from here. I want to know what was in that truck." The manager practically lost the cigarette dangling from his mouth and stared wide-eyed at Eric. Something seemed to catch in his throat. Eric surmised it was the truth. Finally, the man attempted a feeble excuse that he didn't know what Eric was talking about.

Eric produced a tablet with the video loaded on it. "I can tell you exactly from which storage tank the truck gained its load, and I can show you exactly where it ended up. Now, let's not play dodge-the-truth games here. I can go immediately to the state and turn this video over to them. I suspect your operation might come to a screeching halt with that information."

The man stared incredulously at Eric. Then he dropped his gaze and started to talk. "We . . . I mean I hired an outside contractor to dispose of our waste product. We . . . I mean I didn't really check out where the contractor was taking the stuff."

"Of course, you didn't! Why would you? You knew it was a slop job from the start given how much they charge to do the dirty work. I imagine you saved quite a bundle as opposed to a legitimate trucking company that would dispose of it properly."

Eric knew he nailed the manager squarely where it hurt. He had no defense and gave up. "What do you want?"

"I'm obligated to notify the state of this impropriety. However, I want to nail the Overshoot gang firmly to the wall. They're a dangerous group, and I need all the information I can dig up on them. I'll need a detailed statement from you acknowledging this illegal transaction. Include any names of people you dealt with. It must be notarized and signed by your company's proper representatives."

The manager knew he could do nothing but agree to Eric's request. Some clemency might be given to his company if they cooperated in bringing down Overshoot Mining. The papers would be prepared and available in a couple days.

Next, Eric met up with Joseph and together they visited the chemical plant's main office armed with video proof of misdoings. They met with the same response as the fertilizer manager. *These guys are in no way prepared to deal with anyone finding out about their crimes.* Eventually, an agreement was reached, and Eric felt they were on their way to closing a very nasty, toxic-waste dumping operation.

But this story doesn't stop with dumping waste. There're murders to account for. Illegal disposal is one thing, but that doesn't deal with the deaths of killers and innocent citizens. There has to be more involved than illegal waste disposal; but what?

Outside the chemical plant, Eric and Joseph talked. Eric said, "Both companies agreed to suspend disposing waste via illegal methods. They'll bite the financial bullet and contract with legitimate truckers to deal with their toxic residues."

"Looks like a clean sweep!" said Joseph.

"Of course, there may be other companies involved. It'll be up to the State to see if they can find other industries involved in the Overshoot scheme and inspect other Overshoot enterprises. We've got bigger problems to solve. Murder is our top agenda."

Eric and Joseph stopped at a small café for an afternoon break. They mulled over their next move. Eric said, "Proving illegal dumping is one thing, but murder and a falsified will and contract account for much more. Overshoot'll be slapped with a severe fine and ordered to clean up the site, but at the same time they might go free of more heinous crimes. That trap can't be sprung until we've got proof."

They discussed how to prove Overshoot Mining was behind the killings. Joseph yawned, "Eric, I think we need a plan, but what?"

"Still working on it. Let's go back to the office."

As the pair exited the café, a hail of bullets sprayed the ground around them. Eric dodged to the left and Joseph to the right to confuse whoever owned the gun or guns. During the first volley, one bullet grazed Joseph's arm and another skimmed Eric's leg. Both wounds began to bleed. Ducking behind parked cars, they recognized two sources of automatic rifle fire penetrating cars in front of them. If one bullet punctured a gas tank, things could become unpleasant.

Being pinned down, it was too dangerous to try and shoot it out. *Glocks versus high powered rifles? Too lopsided in the criminals' favor.* They crouched low and retreated from the parking lot while keeping cars between themselves and gunfire. The café sat in a dense wooded area. This provided cover for whoever did the shooting but also allowed Eric and Joseph to find an escape route.

Once far enough out of sight, Joseph and Eric worked their way around behind their adversaries. Silently moving from tree to tree to outflank whoever fired the shots, Eric and Joseph noticed the gunfire slowed. Perhaps the gunmen waited for movement from behind the cars. *Guess they didn't see us escape because of the trees.* Joseph and Eric moved toward the rear of the gunmen.

A wide loop brought them up behind the persons of interest. Two men crouched behind a hedge. They were intent on watching the autos vacated by Eric and Joseph. The men spoke in low voices. "What's we gonna do now? Did we kill 'em?"

"Dunno. Maybe. We waits to see, ya know? Could be playin' 'possum."

"I'm fir givin' 'em some more; maybe flush 'em out." He raised his weapon to fire.

Eric and Joseph were in position behind the crooks. They drew their Glocks, pointed them at the men, and shouted, "Drop your weapons, now!" The criminals were so surprised they obeyed. Staff at the café had phoned the sheriff's office. In minutes after the capture, deputies pulled up and arrested the would-be assassins. Questioning revealed they were specifically hired to kill Eric and Joseph.

"We was contracted taday and was told where ta find ya. Yea, we works out of a cellphone. Da guy who hires us pays cash at a post box."

Eric said to Joseph, "It looks like one or both of our offending companies tipped off the Overshoots. Neither of these guys knows their employer. Everything is anonymous. Cash transfer covers their financial tracks."

Joseph said, "Their employer is shrewd. Nothing leads back to the Overshoot company."

Eric nodded his head glumly. "Another capture, and we're no closer to pinning the worst crimes on Overshoot Mining. Why'd the rain of bullets come so soon after our surveillance? The chemical and fertilizer companies and the Overshoots must be tied together tighter than we thought."

Both Eric and Joseph felt stymied. EMTs arrived and patched up Joseph and Eric. Their wounds were superficial but painful.

"Let's take the rest of the day off and think how to proceed."

Joseph agreed. Eric considered Sarah his favorite sounding board. He called her. After chiding him for being in a shootout, she said, "Of course, I can meet you to talk. Tell me where and I'm there right after work."

Both Joseph and Eric returned to their homes. *These wounds are building up all over my body! I'm so glad I've got a nurse next door to keep me patched up. Those thugs ruined a good pair of pants too!*

After getting cleaned up and visiting his neighborhood "health care provider", Eric drove to meet Sarah. He pulled into the restaurant's parking lot and saw Sarah waiting by her car. Even though she spent a full day working in the law office, she still looked stunning. Eric sighed. *I really want a lifelong relationship with this woman.*

Sarah noticed his slight limp. "Did you get hurt?"

Shrugging, he said, "Well, Joseph and I were ambushed, and each got a graze. They're superficial, but I do feel mine a bit."

Sarah's nostrils flared, but she took a deep breath before speaking. "This only adds to my concern for your safety. I want a full report on this latest attempt on your life!"

"I know. I need to be more careful."

Sarah shook her head and said, "You don't know how awful these stories make me feel. I practically pray all day long for your safety. That's the only thing that keeps me from going nuts with worry."

Not sensing what else to say, Eric replied, "I know it's terrible not knowing if or when I'll show up. Will I arrive with a smile or be full of bullet holes?" His attempt at humor fell on serious ears. *Bad attempt! She can't laugh about this!*

Sarah's tear ducts overflowed, and she reached for a tissue to blot her eyes.

"I'm sorry. I'm so crass. I just don't know what to say."

"It . . . it's okay. My emotions are too close to the edge right now." She breathed a deep sigh and looked at Eric with concerned love.

The tense moment finally passed, and they tried to think of options to find evidence that would put the Overshoot group behind bars. Eric decided a frontal attack might be best. Sarah disliked Eric's direct methods, but she knew they often seemed to work. Eric phoned Joseph, and they talked for fifteen minutes about how to work the plan. After Eric hung up, he turned to Sarah. She was toying with the remains of a salad.

"Being with you releases so many great ideas . . ." Then Eric caught himself and added, with enthusiasm, ". . . not the least of which is how much I want to be with you for . . . well, you know!"

Sarah smiled broadly, revealing well-polished teeth. She knew Eric tried hard to keep their relationship at the forefront. *In his own way, he has a romantic flare. I know what he means; but his words don't sound like something from a romance novel.*

"Remind me of our next counseling session."

"Tomorrow afternoon, same as our first one."

On arriving at his apartment, Eric felt his bandages might need checking; he knocked on Alice's apartment door.

"You're sure keeping me busy," the nurse said. "Explain again how you got this one?"

Eric explained with more detail. After her handiwork, he headed for bed. Another night of not being able to find a comfortable position was ahead. *Too many dings in all the wrong places!*

Chapter 19

The next day was attack time for Eric and Joseph. They drove in Joseph's car to the Overshoot mine, or should it be called the McDonnell mine?

Joseph commented, "Our plan might work."

"Let's hope so." Eric felt a tinge of doubt.

As they approached the mine site, Eric breathed a prayer for their mutual wisdom and safety. Both would be needed. The guard at the entrance needed to know what they wanted.

"We've got business with the mine manager and must see him in person."

After a phone call, and several minutes, they were invited to the site office, a modified travel trailer. *Pretty low-brow shack for a company that must be in a very lucrative business. Keeps the overhead down, I guess.*

The manager was a short and thick individual who looked like he ate nails for breakfast, washed down with vinegar. His introduction matched his appearance, "Whadda ya want?"

"We're curious private investigators. And our curiosity hasn't gone unnoticed by your company. It seems a chemical company and a fertilizer manufacturing facility hired your company to dump toxic wastes on this property illegally. We're here to inspect the waste site. It's part of the report we're preparing for the State. We expect that you won't have a job by the time those folks check things out here."

The manager jumped from his chair ready to do battle. Then he thought better of it, took a deep breath, and asked for proof. Eric showed him the video of waste being picked up and then dumped at the mine. He seemed to simmer down after seeing the visual evidence. Following some stammering, he asked if he could make a call to his boss.

"Great! I would love to speak with your boss."

The manager balked at this and said the man above him might be out of town and couldn't be reached.

"Humm. That's funny. You were going to call him a minute ago, but now he's unavailable. Very interesting. Let's cut the lies and go for the truth. Take us to the waste site right now!" The manager could hardly deny the request at this point. He doffed a hard hat and motioned for Eric and Joseph to do the same.

They walked some distance over the property before reaching the dump. "Do you have a copy of that video I could have?" asked the manager.

Eric knew he wanted to see if there were additional copies or if Eric had the original with him. "Oh, I never depend on one copy of anything. Too dangerous when one deals with murderers who have no heart, wipe out family members, and try to murder us."

The manager swallowed hard and kept walking. His bristle was subdued.

"You see," continued Eric, "if we don't check in every hour, not only will the State Attorney General's office and Mr. Sean McDonnell's attorneys be notified, but this place will be crawling with some very unhappy state police."

The manager's eyes widened, and he began to stammer. "I . . . I . . . I'm a flunky for this outfit. I just see that the trucks come and do their thing and go."

"That's known as an accomplice after the fact. You're as close to the trigger as anyone, I suspect. When did the fertilizer manager call you about our little visit?"

"I . . . I . . . can't say."

"I'll bet you can't! Your boss would leave your body beside a deserted road if you said anything."

At this point, sweat began to soak through the manager's clothes, and it wasn't from walking. He had no idea how to handle the situation.

"Is that the dump site?" asked Joseph, pointing to a light-colored area at one end of the "mine."

"Ye . . . Yes."

Just then, a truck bearing gifts for the site approached. The driver went right to the site and began unloading his prize. Eric recorded every move the driver made.

"I like this," Eric said. "My video will be excellent material to show the state authorities. Shall I include you in the recording?" The manager turned away, covered his face, and refused to look at the camera. "Well, we thank you for your hospitality, and I hope you provide your superiors with a fine narrative of our visit. Good day."

And with that remark, Eric and Joseph gave their hard hats to the manager and walked to Joseph's pickup.

"Will they try to kill us here?" wondered Joseph under his breath.

"I don't think so. They'll wait until we're on neutral ground. We'll have to keep our guard up."

They got into the vehicle and cautiously turned on the engine. No bomb! Joseph eased away from the Overshoot dump site, glad to be away from the operation.

"What now?" asked Joseph.

"I guess we wait for developments." He really didn't know what to do until Overshoot Mining made their next move. They had planned to hit the chemical and fertilizer managers next, but Eric felt it might be best to postpone that confrontation. After all, he had no proof those companies tipped off Overshoot.

"The thing that bothers me most is why these people are so focused on this site that they resort to murder and hired assassins to rub out everyone who gets in their way. There must be other locations just as good as this one to dump waste. I think we should do a little more geology before we stir up the hornets' nest any more than it is."

They drove to their office and began some serious online searches of geological databases. After an hour of trying all sorts of key words, Joseph yelled, "Bingo!" Eric rushed to his friend's monitor to see what he found. A mild-mannered man, Joseph rarely got excited about anything. "Look at this!" Joseph gushed.

The screen held a scanned copy of an old Arkansas Geological Survey study of this section of the Magnet Cove area. Joseph pulled up the digitized image of a frayed looking map of the region. McDonnell's farm sat prominently on the map. Lots of symbols illustrated test sites where the author took samples. Several symbols indicated mineral deposits of some sort. Unfortunately, the smudged markings could not be read. Eric clicked through the pages, trying to find details about the samples. After a great deal of looking, a page with the correct location of samples popped up.

Joseph asked, "What did the author discover on the farm?"

"I don't know. But words by the sample numbers indicate nothing was analyzed. It looks like the specimens are gathering dust in the state geological survey's warehouse. We've got to go see what those samples are!"

With a quick goodbye to Megan, they dashed out the door with a copy of the article loaded on a small computer. Driving to the survey office and warehouse in Little Rock, Eric hoped these specimens were not pitched out by some overzealous administrator trying to make space for the latest equipment needed to bring the Survey up to speed. The pace of technology related to the work of the Arkansas State Geological Survey required continuous updating of lab and field equipment.

They parked in the Survey's lot and walked into the main office. A receptionist on duty smiled and said, "How can ah help you, Dr. Bonfield and Mr. Hernandez?" Eric showed her the Survey reference and asked if they could look for the samples of interest.

"I think y'all need to see Frank Smit, our staff geologist who takes care of archived materials. I'll ring 'im." After a brief phone conversation, she said, "If y'all know where the warehouse's located, try the side door. Frank'll be there."

Frank Smit waited by the door when they arrived. Eric knew him as an efficient person with a flair for order and a brilliant red beard. His plaid shirt and field jacket loaded with various items made him stand out in a crowd as a geologist.

"Great to see you, Eric and Joseph. I've been followin' your exploits in the news. Looks like you get to use your gun as a regular part of your field equipment." He laughed.

"I'd much rather use a rock hammer and a hand lens. But gotta do what you gotta do." He also laughed.

They walked into the warehouse. "As you see, we're gettin' full. Several the oil companies gave us their sample logs. That takes up a lot of space. We're doin' what we can to rearrange so we can store everything. We never know when a citizen or company needs specific samples found only in our archives."

"This is a very important service. And we're here with just that type of request."

Eric gave Frank the Survey reference and asked to see samples from Abe's farm site. Smit punched some identifiers into a computer. The display indicated a location where the samples might be found. He led Eric and Joseph past huge stacks of boxes and files. In a remote location, Frank found and pulled out a very old and musty smelling field box.

"Let's see what this holds," said Eric as he opened the box with excited hands. Inside sat several cloth bags at the point of deterioration. "Can we look at these with a binocular microscope and do some tests?"

"No problem. The lab's just down the next aisle."

Frank took them to an analytical lab with an impressive array of equipment. Eric was ecstatic. He carefully unwrapped the first bag from the McDonnell farmstead. Bright red crystals glared at his eyes. Eric didn't need to do any tests. He immediately recognized the mineral. It was *vanadinite.*

Frank whistled and said, "Nice catch, Eric! Those are some pretty ones."

"So that's what they're really after," said Eric. "Joseph, this valuable mineral is an important source for the element vanadium, used in steel manufacture. It has many industrial uses, such as making jet engines, high-speed aircraft, superconducting magnets, ceramics and as a catalyst to produce sulfuric acid." He opened other bags. All contained beautiful crystals of vanadinite. "McDonnell's place must have a rich ore of this stuff. Surely the Overshoot people know this. Thanks for finding this, Frank. Since these are evidence involved in a murder investigation, they should be under lock and key."

"No problem. Glad to help with one of your cases. Let me put these in a better box so you can take them with you." Frank signed out the specimens to Eric as evidence to be stored at the police station.

"Before we leave, could you check your log to see if anyone else has asked to look at this collection of samples?"

Smit went to his computer and punched some keys. "Somebody named Jones asked about the specimens." The date preceded the Overshoot gang's attempt to take over the McDonnell property. "According to the computer entry, whoever made the request didn't actually visit the Survey. They just wanted to know that the specimens existed. Said they'd be by later. Haven't showed up yet."

"These guys must have known some geology or at least knew enough to search survey files to look for important commodities locations. They didn't just stumble onto McDonnell's property.

Theirs is a deliberate attempt to gain control of a known ore body without anyone knowing about the vanadium."

Joseph said, "Since we didn't see any vanadinite when we visited the site, I'll bet they're dumping waste at a location removed from where these samples came from. The dump is just a sidebar to future exploitation of vanadium ore."

"Bing! And I'm sure you're right. I'd better phone the police to request an escort to the station. We don't want to take any chances with these special bits of evidence."

A patrol car arrived at the warehouse door and the sample box was placed in a special locked container residing in the vehicle's trunk. The car drove off with Eric and Joseph following close behind. They were barely out of the Survey's parking lot before a burst of gunfire interrupted their trip.

Bullets riddled the officer's car, striking him. He lost control, bounced over a ditch, and smashed into a tree. Eric shouted into his cell phone for backup. Additional police were on patrol not far away. The stricken car's violent embrace of the tree ruptured the gas tank and fuel spewed to the ground.

"Be careful! If the wrong bullet strikes metal, that car'll go up in flames!"

Eric and Joseph were only a short distance behind and swerved to avoid a collision. Bullets began to strike their car. They quickly backed up, leaped from their vehicle, and dodged behind a stone fence for cover.

"We can't let them get those specimens," yelled Eric.

They drew their Glocks and split up, seeking hiding places while they approached the officer and his wrecked car. Rifle fire blew out the officer's tires, but the shooters seemed careful to avoid starting a fire. *They want the samples undamaged.* One man dashed toward the vehicle. Eric and Joseph opened fire. He went down, screaming in pain. This brought more shots from others concealed in nearby trees.

Joseph and Eric chose places that shielded them from the hail of bullets. This neighborhood had ornate stone fences which afforded good cover. The gun battle continued. Eric estimated there were at least two sources of the bullets. He signaled Joseph to keep up the firing in a delaying action until reinforcements arrived. That didn't take long. Sirens wailed and converged from two directions.

The assailants realized their problem and made one last desperate attempt to reach the crashed car. With one of them pouring lead toward Joseph and Eric, the other ran toward the vehicle. Eric knew their game and carefully aimed through a crack in the wall. He squeezed off two rounds from his Glock, and the man crumpled to the ground. Knowing they failed, the other gunman stopped firing, jumped from his tree, and ran. Joseph's expert aim easily took the gunman down.

Police officers swarmed the site, collected guns, and corralled the injured. None were badly hurt, and all would survive to face attempted murder charges in court. Fortunately, the stricken officer didn't have life-threatening wounds.

After giving testimony to officers, Eric and Joseph inspected their vehicle for bullet holes. The minor damage could be repaired. They took possession of the locked box from the immobile patrol car, moved it to their vehicle, and drove to evidence storage at the station.

Later, police informed Eric that the three hired gunmen provided no more information than others Eric and Joseph had captured. It was the same story. An anonymous person hired them to do a job. Still no direct connection to Overshoot Mining. *When will the missing link appear?*

Eric said to Joseph, "Things are moving toward a climax, I guess. Sooner or later a crack opens and exposes the bad guys. Problem is I've no idea how to pry open the crack." He smiled grimly.

After securing the evidence box at police headquarters, Joseph and Eric drove downtown to let Sean McDonnell know about the evidence they gathered for his team of attorneys.

McDonnell was finishing a meeting when the pair walked into his office, a bit rumpled from their shootout.

"You guys look a sight! What happened?"

After hearing their explanation, Sean said, "Good work. But I'm worried for your lives. These people are killers. How'll you pin these murders and attempted murders on the Overshoot bunch? There's only enough evidence to shut down the site because of dumping toxic waste."

"I'm afraid you're right," said Eric. "The company is liable for contaminating the aquifer or aquifers that serve groundwater to farms around the McDonnell property. Joseph's water well analysis data confirmed that those chemicals are all coming from the dump site. The chemical and fertilizer companies will face huge fines. The coerced signing of the contract and the will allotting control of mineral rights to Overshoot Mining is moving closer to being proved. But I've a nagging uncertainty that highly paid lawyers can argue away our evidence."

Sean, Joseph, and Eric all stared into space, uncertain how to move forward. Eric said, "We need someone from the Overshoot gang to spill the truth. That'd destroy the Overshoot's claim and put people in jail. It'd demolish the careers of crooked lawyers. But we don't have anyone admitting this. Otherwise, how do we connect Overshoot with the murders?"

"Who'd be most likely to squeal on the organization?"

"Aside from the paralegal, who no longer works for Overshoot Mining, I only know two people who work below the CEO: the manager at the mine site and Sam Beechtree, the crooked lawyer. The manager sits low on the food chain and is unlikely to provide much convincing evidence about the will and contract." Sean and Joseph nodded agreement.

"The most likely person is the lawyer. He's got a lot to lose if things go south. His license to practice law in Arkansas would be forfeited, and a possible jail sentence might be his lot. Maybe it's time to put some pressure on Beechtree. But I'm tired and the day is about over. Besides, Sarah and I have a date with our counselor."

Joseph and Sean felt they could go no further until Eric tried to put the squeeze on Sam Beechtree. The meeting broke up.

Chapter 20

At the counseling session Elaine welcomed them and, after pleasantries, spent a half hour going over her findings, based on evaluations they filled out. There were positives, which Elaine praised. Other areas clearly needed work. Their positives included common religious faith, sense of morality, desire to see the other person's point of view, shared value of money and how to use it, view of each other as whole persons, and openness to communicate.

The other side of the story involved family backgrounds, value of time spent together (Sarah wished for more time spent one-on-one with Eric), uncertainty about how work and home should be valued, dangers associated with Eric's work, uncertainty about having children, and, to a some extent, their personalities. Sarah's first-born position and Eric's middle child family location were points of contention. Sarah and Eric listened with fascination at how well Elaine could see the issues they faced. Elaine laughed and blamed the computer.

After describing the pluses and concerns, Elaine asked, "How committed are you to work on your areas of disagreement."

Eric and Sarah looked at each other and said, almost in unison, "We want to work on them!"

"Change is never simple or easy. I'm giving you an assignment to work on between now and our next session."

They thanked Elaine, paid her fee, and went out to dinner. Twirling his pasta, Eric said, "What do you think?"

Sarah arched her brow and nodded. "The ball's in our court. Elaine wants us to work on the questions separately and then come together and share our thinking."

"Intuitively, I'd think just talking things out together would save time, but she's got the sheepskin on the wall. Besides, what do I know except rocks and crime?" Eric laughed when he said this, and Sarah chuckled too.

She gave him a sly smile and said, "I think you know a whole lot more than rocks and crime. You've got the most brilliant mind of anyone I've ever known." At this she reached out her hand and squeezed his. Her eyes penetrated his and Eric felt she was looking into his soul.

"Wow. I don't know quite what to say after that one! I'm supposed to return the compliment, but your words leave me speechless."

Sarah smiled and said, "That's the first time I've ever heard you respond without saying something clever. I'll have to remember this." And with that she picked up a pea with her spoon and catapulted it toward him. In shock, Eric instinctively grabbed the pea and tossed it back. They played dodgeball with the pea until it wore out and splattered on his cheek.

"Now, I've got something to say," he announced. "Anyone who leaves me speechless is the person I want in my corner through all the battles of life. Now top that one!"

Sarah buckled over with laughter and threw another pea. Then she looked around and saw that other couples were staring at them wide-eyed and smiling. At this she dropped her eyes to her plate and announced in a profound, but low voice, "I think we might want to continue this discussion elsewhere."

Equally austere, Eric said, with a grim face, "Of course, my dear. Let us display decorum." They laughed again and waved to the nearby couples, who waved back. Dinner concluded with more laughter. They agreed it was time to break up the party and work on their assignments.

Chapter 21

"I'm headed to the law office of Sam Beechtree," Eric told Megan. "Going to confront the lion in his lair."

Megan nodded and said, "A prayer's coming your way!"

Eric smiled and said, "Thanks. I really need that!"

Beachtree's office was in one of the taller buildings in downtown Little Rock. *Pretty nice digs! Rent for this place must be out of sight.*

Sam Beechtree's secretary was away from her desk, so Eric knocked on the lawyer's inner office. Beechtree sat up wide-eyed, gulped at seeing Eric, and said, "What . . . what do you want?"

"Mr. Beechtree, I think you're fully appraised of our visit to the McDonnell dump site and the evidence we've documented about illegal deposition of toxic waste there. We've got plenty of evidence that farm wells around the site are contaminated by the very chemicals being dumped at the site. This is enough to shut down the facility and cause considerable financial harm to Overshoot Mining operations.

"We also have evidence the real reason for Overshoot Mining wanting the site is the extraction of vanadium. This is information the company didn't provide to the state. The State of Arkansas will be very displeased with this. I'm certain you're fully aware of the illegality of the will and contract supposedly signed by Mr. McDonnell. We have evidence this was forced on a very ill and momentarily incompetent Abe McDonnell. Such incompetence nullifies the will, by state law. Further, the murders of Paul McDonnell, Hugh Fogel, and Mr. McDonnell's physician can only be directed toward the Overshoot operation. In addition, the attempted killing of me, my associate, a police officer, Josephine McDonnell, and Mr. Sean McDonnell all point to this company, which you represent. You, Mr. Beechtree, are right in the middle of this mess and face, at a minimum, loss of licensure, disbarment, and felonious activity. Perhaps even murder can be pinned on you."

Eric paused to breathe. Beechtree stared in stunned silence at Eric; he tried to absorb the certainty of these accusations.

"If I were you, I think I'd start singing like a canary and expose the parties responsible for this murderous and evil plot. You might, just might, receive a lesser sentence than if you keep silent. I'm not in a position to cut any deals, but I'd be prepared when you face the State's attorneys."

Sam Beechtree looked down at the floor as his mind ran over options. Eric gave him plenty of time. Sam slowly began to speak, "There's a lot you can pin on me, but murder isn't one. I had nothing to do with that side of the equation. Yes, I can expose the principles responsible for everything I was in on, but killing people wasn't in my agreement with Overshoot." He paused and wiped his forehead with a tissue. "I've been waiting for this shoe to drop and now it has. We'd better go before I break down in my own office. I want to talk to the District Attorney."

Beechtree and Eric walked to Eric's rental car. "Sorry, but my regular wheels are sitting in a garage. It's waiting for them to fix bullet holes delivered courtesy of you-know-who."

Sam Beechtree nodded grimly. The passenger side door squeaked in protest as Sam opened it. As he turned to enter the car, a bullet shot through the air, grazing his skull. Eric yanked the dazed man into his car, pulled the door shut, and stepped on the gas. The sad excuse for a vehicle hurtled away from the assassin's gun as the engine sputtered and coughed from exertion.

After several turns to put them at a safe distance from the shooter, Eric pulled to the roadside and looked at Beechtree's wound. Sam showed panic symptoms.

"We'd better do something to stop the bleeding." Eric grabbed a first aid kit and had Beechtree apply pressure with a wad of gauze. "That should slow the flow of blood." After a few minutes, Sam stopped gasping for breath and sighed.

"I should've known the Overshoot bunch would bug my office." He said this between deep breaths.

"Must be! I don't see how they'd know what's going on otherwise. I have to get you to the D.A. pronto. Maybe she can put you into some sort of protection program. These guys don't play nice."

Sam nodded. "I wanted out of the Overshoot system but didn't know how to manage it without getting killed. Those people will stop at nothing to achieve their ends. I hope this gives me a way to escape. Otherwise, I'm a marked man."

Eric pushed the ancient car faster. *Got to get Sam into some sort of protection.* When they reached the District Attorney's office, Eric inspected the wound. After a little first aid, Beechtree was ready to spill what he knew. Equipment was hurriedly set up for his testimony to be witnessed and videotaped, legally. After an hour's worth of taping Sam describing the ins and outs of Overshoot Mining, Eric felt he had some of his questions answered. Names and details verified that Mr. Abe McDonnell was certainly incompetent to sign the will and contract giving mineral rights to Overshoot. Abe's inability to know what he was signing was clearly due to ingestion of a toxic chemical administered at the restaurant sessions.

Beechtree finally admitted that it was he who slipped the chemical into Abe's drink. Eric beamed at this break in the case. "I didn't know it would eventually kill him. The CEO gave me the chemical each time we met. I tried to avoid being taped by Fogel when I actually put the stuff in Abe's glass."

Eric laid out evidence of waste being dumped on Abe's farm and subsequent contamination of an important aquifer providing water to nearby farms. The D.A. said she would begin proceedings to shut down the operation and start legal action against all parties involved.

Beechtree also provided the names of additional companies using Overshoot's services to dump wastes at other sites in the state. Some of Overshoot Mining's dumps might become superfund sites if the dimensions proved great enough. Hopefully, waste could be dug up and properly disposed of. Cleaning up aquifers would be another matter. Purging toxic materials from groundwater is extremely expensive and time-consuming. Eric doubted the Overshoot group's ability to foot the bill. They would face bankruptcy. The crooks involved could face hefty prison terms.

Eric said, "I wish we could attach murder charges to whoever ordered the killings by Overshoot henchmen."

The D.A. agreed, but they knew the evidence was insufficient to implicate company officials, whoever they might be. So far, circumstantial evidence ruled.

Then Eric had an idea. *What if I push a major player in Overshoot Mining to make an overt move to kill me? I'd be in danger, but it might work.*

"Ma'am, I have a thought about how to draw these people out into the open." He talked the idea over with the D.A.

"What you say might work, but I'm very reluctant to put you in the line of fire."

"I know it's a dangerous proposition, but I can't come up with anything better right now. For it to work, I'll need electronic gear, phone taps, and serious backup."

"I can provide all that," she said, as she sat back in her chair and rubbed her temples. "But I still don't feel comfortable putting you in harm's way."

It took Eric an hour to convince the D.A. he'd be okay. *At least I hope so. I can only control my own self, not what a criminal'll do.* He pushed these thoughts aside and began to scratch out his plan on a piece of paper. If his idea worked, it might just smoke out the true company villains. He knew any results would come with a big "if." *I feel most confident if Joseph can do what I'm sure he can do. I've got to talk with him.*

Eric phoned Joseph and they talked for half an hour.

"You know you're putting your life in my hands, don't you?" Joseph said.

"Exactly. That's why I'm asking you to consider doing this. I wouldn't trust anyone else to do this job. You've got the skill and you've never failed me yet!"

"Whew! That puts a lot of pressure on this frail person!"

"I don't consider you frail. Remember those times you bailed me out? I've got full confidence in you!"

"If you say so."

"I say so!"

"Alright. I'll do it. I'll need the right equipment."

"You'll have it. The D.A. promised."

As Eric drove to his apartment, he felt good about the plan but knew it might freak out Sarah. *What would she think about me doing this? What should I do? Is it easier to ask for forgiveness after the deed is done or tell her what I plan to do?*

Then Eric thought of what Elaine said at their most recent counseling session. "Be honest with each other." Her words penetrated him. They echoed through his brain. Eric knew if he and Sarah were going to share their lives together, he must begin now to let her in on this, his most dangerous plan. Reluctantly, he phoned her and asked if they could have a quick supper and talk.

"Why, of course!"

Talking is our strong suit. He smiled at this. Then his face showed the grooves of a frown. *How should I bring up the subject?* He laughed. *Don't I always start off my conversations with the facts?* He wasn't one to beat around the bush. *I'll go right up to her, hold her in my arms, and kiss her.* Then he would break the news. *Now, if I just have the guts to do this!*

When Eric saw Sarah, he started to follow his plan, but doubts began to creep in. *I can't panic now!*

She smiled but immediately picked up on his anxiety. *He needs something!*

Mustering his strength, he said, "Sarah, I want you to know that I'm facing a very dangerous situation, but it may resolve this case and catch the bad guys."

I knew it! Sarah's face grew serious, but she continued to smile as she listened.

After he finished, she stared at the sidewalk but saw none of it. After a long moment, Sarah lifted her head and her gaze penetrated Eric's eyes. She nodded solemnly and said, "Eric. This is a creative idea and a dangerous one, as you say. You must know I'll pray continually for divine protection. I want angels to surround you in such a close flock that nothing can penetrate their protective shroud. I believe in you and want you to come back here and hold me just as you will tonight. Is that a deal?"

What a woman! He felt so much relief that he lifted Sarah into the air and held her there. "Oh, I'll be back; I'll be back! You can count on it!"

Chapter 22

Eric rose early, ate his breakfast with determination, and readied his mind for an assault on the Overshoot kingdom. He checked in with Joseph. Without Eric's partner, the plan would never work. "Are you up for this?"

Eric could almost see the twinkle in Joseph's eyes as he listened to his partner. "My friend, I've never been more ready for anything in my life. I can't wait to do my part."

Eric smiled, too, and closed the connection. Then he methodically called the state police and various forensic specialists. Things were moving toward a climax, although he wasn't certain exactly what the climax might look like. Nervously, Eric cleaned and rechecked his Glock. Two extra magazines rested comfortably in his jacket. *No clue how many I'll need. Hopefully none. That would be nice.* His jacket also bore a tiny phone. It was so small he had a hard time keeping track of it. Eric breathed deeply. *I'm as ready as I'll ever be.* The last thing he did was the most important: he prayed.

Eric drove to Overshoot Mining headquarters. In the parking lot, Eric called the state police commander in charge of the operation. "I'm ready."

"So are we," said the major.

Surveillance indicated Alfred Franklin, the main kingpin, would be in his office. Franklin and Eric had confronted each other in the restaurant where everything about this case began. *That meeting led to today's pinnacle moment.* He parked in a visitor's space and walked to the building's front entrance. A guard asked for I.D. and Eric produced it.

The guard spoke into a phone and nodded his head. He pointed a boney finger and said, "Up the stairs and to the right."

Why didn't the guard frisk me? Maybe he's distracted by my I.D. Marching up the stairs, he proceeded with trepidation to his rendezvous with destiny. *It's one thing to lay out a plan, but plans can go south very fast.*

He counted the number of steps in the staircase. *Never know when a quick exit with the lights out might be necessary.* He knocked on an imposing door that read, "Alfred Franklin, Chief Executive Officer". He was greeted by a beautiful blonde receptionist wearing a short skirt and low-cut top. She spoke to her boss on the intercom in a seductive voice and called him Al. *I doubt she was chosen for the job because of her secretarial skills.* She escorted Eric to an inner office with an imposing and ornate door.

Eric stepped into a spacious room with exotic décor. He did a quick survey of windows and exits, although he had memorized the general room layout from building plans. *These decorations must've set the company back some serious change.*

"Ah, Mr. Bonfield. We met at the restaurant," was the CEO's calm greeting.

"Yes, I'm the man you've tried hard to kill several times. But your goons haven't been successful. Where do you pick up such misfits of society?"

Alfred Franklin wasn't used to anyone speaking so straightforwardly to him. His face turned red and his eyes burned with rage. His breath came in short gasps. Then he took a deep breath and fought to gain control. He said nothing.

"You're aware of the evidence I've accumulated on your sleazy company, if one can call it a company. Murder, Inc. is perhaps a better name than Overshoot Mining. It seems to me you have *overshot* your mark by quite a bit, Mr. Franklin. I've got the names of your slinky group in my pocket. You're all going down. Overshoot Mining will shatter into little bits and pieces. Better turn yourself in."

Franklin started to speak, but Eric continued, "Denial is useless. I know your game. Stop playing it, and you might have a little leniency from the courts. The only words I want to hear from you are words of penance."

At this, Franklin seemed to develop an evil calm. His facial demeanor began to glow as a devilish grin crept across his mouth. He reached for an office phone and said, "Judy? Please tell my assistant to take care of Mr. Bonfield. He's become thoroughly annoying. And don't leave any part of the body able to be identified."

Well, this is what I wanted, but now what? The office door opened, and a hulk of a man entered with his gun drawn. Eric had rehearsed the whole scene before in his mind. He leaped over Franklin's desk and grabbed the CEO's neck in a vise grip. Just then, a shot broke the silence. The window of Franklin's office shattered into a thousand pieces, and the thug dropped to the floor.

Good old Joseph. His partner was positioned to see the interior of the office. Eric had only recently learned that Joseph was in the

Mexican army before immigrating to the United States. He'd been a sniper with a special ops group.

"And now, Mr. Franklin, would you like to do what I suggested, or do you want to try something else equally stupid?"

Franklin's eyes were bulging from the pressure of Eric's arm on his neck. He gurgled a "NO!"

Eric relaxed his grip just enough for Franklin to lunge backward. This threw Eric off balance and against the wall behind the desk. Franklin proved to be a powerfully built person. He turned and swung his fist at Eric's stomach, knocking the wind out of him. Freed from Eric's grip, Franklin dashed for the door, hurtling over the body of his henchman. By the time Eric regained his breath, Franklin had disappeared.

Eric shouted into his phone as he ran out the door. "Major, Franklin's gone. Better hurry."

State police surrounding the building came running in. They dispatched the guard as they took control of the facility.

The State Police Major ran up the stairs and joined Eric. "We've got his other hired thugs and staff corralled. Where do you think Franklin went?"

"He was so quick I couldn't follow him until I caught my breath."

A state police officer charged up to report. "Sir, one of the ranking staff told me that Franklin escaped by a hidden tunnel known only to a few in the company."

"Let's see who we've bagged," said the major.

A tally showed everyone on the list given by Sam Beechtree was accounted for except Franklin, his second in command, and the guy who hired the assassins, known as Jimmie or Frank. *Three big ones got away.*

Lesser Overshoot staff began to sing loudly! State police wanted to know where the three big guys might be headed. Lots of opinions were voiced, but the most knowledgeable insiders thought New Orleans was the most likely spot. The bulk of Overshoot's cash sat in one bank. They would empty the company's bank account, split the firm's money, and scatter. That was the escape plan if things fell apart. A company jet sat ready to fly at a moment's notice.

A law enforcement team quickly formed to search for the missing culprits. Eric and Joseph were invited to go along, since they had firsthand knowledge of Franklin. The team dashed for the Little Rock airport, and the race was on. New Orleans bank officials were notified to report the presence of suspicious characters as soon as they came into the bank. Accounts of their size couldn't be emptied except in person.

The airport reported that Overshoot Mining's jet had taken off before police called to stop the fugitives flight. Eric calculated that neither his group nor the escapees could reach the bank much ahead of the other. During the hour and a half flight, they maintained constant contact with New Orleans police watching the bank. Everyone was alert for any developments. Where the criminals would land was unknown. *Perhaps they've got a private field. Surely these guys'll avoid public airports.*

The state police jet streaked through humid air dripping with the opportunity for a thunderstorm. Eric turned to Joseph, "Have your contacts in Mexico had any success finding offshore accounts of Overshoot Mining?"

"No. I heard from them early this morning. They found nothing. My relatives are very good at finding such accounts, so I think the company didn't hide money overseas. These Overshoot guys are amateurs at keeping track of money. They stowed it all in one bank in New Orleans. Not very smart."

"That makes it easier to deal with. I'm really surprised. For all their clever manipulations, this blunder seems a silly one to make. I guess none of them were trained in finance. Everybody sooner or later goofs up."

Even with this apparent financial mistake, Eric feared the gang might slip through the police net. His group landed and dashed into waiting squad cars. When they arrived at the bank, police reported nothing suspicious. Eric wasn't satisfied. He asked each cashier about people inquiring to withdraw funds. One cashier said a wire request to withdraw money from one of the accounts just came through.

"Ah don't know what these gentlemen expected. We never empty a huge account without proper authorization. That usually means a personal visit to the bank."

"Thanks for the information, ma'am. You're doing your job well!"

"We try, sir."

Eric hurriedly reported this to the state police commander. "The gang is surely onto us waiting for them. They won't show up now. With no money, escape is the only thing on their minds."

The major said, "Fortunately, squealing employees gave us alternative plans that top brass might use." They knew of several contingencies.

"Which is the most likely?" Eric asked.

"One informant said the order of escape depended on distance from New Orleans, once they had the money. From the list the staff gave us, it looks as if their first choice might be Indianapolis. The Overshoot hideout is supposed to be in a rundown section of the city where they could lay low."

Everyone raced back to the airport, boarded the state police jet, and flew to Indianapolis. During the two-hour flight, state police alerted local police to surround the building and wait until the Arkansas posse arrived.

Joseph said to Eric, "Whew! I've never had this much airplane flying in my life! We usually travel by car on vacations."

"Get used to it. Indy is but one possible sanctuary for these thugs. We don't know if they'll be there or not. As organized as they seem to be, I wouldn't bet with certainty on any of the locations on that list. It might be a ruse they planned to throw off pursuers."

After landing, they rushed to the site. Cautiously, everyone approached the dilapidated structure. An ancient door was locked but yielded to a crowbar. Each room was searched. Nobody home. From dust accumulated on the floor and furniture, the place hadn't been used for some time.

"Must've been tipped off or they never came here in the first place," said the major. "I wonder if they bypassed Indianapolis to throw us off the scent altogether or to delay us long enough for them to escape."

Eric said, "Could be; what's next?"

"Chicago is on the hideout list and might be the next best choice to search for this trio."

Racing with patrol car lights flashing, the team headed back to the Indianapolis airport.

"What'd I tell you, Joseph? Time to enjoy another flight without attendants to give us snacks!"

Joseph shrugged and sighed. "Remind me to always use a car!"

A quick one-hour flight to the Windy City was slowed down by a thunderstorm. After circling for half an hour, they finally landed. Chicago police were uncertain about the vague address given them. A frantic search brought the Arkansas group to an apartment building near the Loop. It took more time to locate a building attendant who knew which room they were looking for. He unlocked the door, but the room was ransacked.

"Overshoot brass either bypassed this site too or stripped it and left in a hurry," said the state police major. "None of the airports in Indianapolis or Chicago reported an unscheduled flight by their jet. They're either using private airports or they went straight for another city hideout."

The pursuit was running into midnight and everyone was discouraged. Stomachs were growling in protest for lack of nourishment.

"Did the staff give us bad info or was the list created to give them time to escape?" Eric scratched his head.

The major said, "The only city left on my list is Minneapolis. Hopefully, there're no other choices. Let's go. This may be our last chance to nail these guys before they skip the country."

Weary from jet travel, they piled onto the state's jet and sped to Minneapolis. The one-hour trip didn't allow much time to rest. Conversation within the team was minimal. Most were starting to doubt the validity of the list. What if it was a gimmick designed to throw them off the trail? Nobody wanted to believe this, but things were looking grim.

Joseph asked, "What if nobody is home here?"

Eric sighed, "That might be what happens, but I hope not."

After landing, they wearily followed the GPS. It led them to a specific house in the city. Eric said, "This address seems precise, unlike the Chicago hideout. Maybe we'll surprise them."

A small residence in an older part of town sported a large rental SUV parked in front. The rear door was ajar, and boxes were visible in the back. "Looks promising," said the major. The team's spirits lifted. After a knock didn't yield any response, muscle broke the door down. Judges in each city had cleared the way with warrants. Inside, many boxes and gear were stacked on tables but not yet sealed for shipment.

"Looks like we arrived in time to crash the party. But where're the party-goers?" Eric said.

A quick survey of the house yielded nobody home. Then Joseph found a false bookcase. "I think this may help us." He pushed on one side and the bookcase rotated to reveal a concealed a hideout where three men huddled together.

"Going somewhere?" asked Eric. Franklin and the other two sighed and knew it was over.

Cuffed and read their rights, the threesome was shipped back to Little Rock aboard the state police jet. Limited seating required Eric and Joseph to catch a commercial flight back home.

Once in state police headquarters, the questioning process began in earnest. The second-in-command broke first and blamed the murders on Franklin and the assassin hiring specialist, Jimmie or Frank. His real name was Howard. Testimonies by Overshoot staff would eventually occupy a huge file, ripe for court use.

Later revelations explained the details. Howard contacted the first set of shooters directly. However, he soon realized the implication if they were caught and squealed on the company. So, company policy developed that any thug with knowledge of their employer would be eliminated, if confronted by the law, regardless of their success or failure on a job. Knowledge of this black-widow-spider approach quickly spread through the criminal community. The number of applicants dropped dramatically.

Howard had to increase the fees. He shifted to anonymous cell phone contacts and payments via post office boxes. This kept Jimmie or Frank from being traced directly. Without the threat of being killed by the company, the number of criminal-for-hire applicants increased. But the qualities and abilities of the ruffians did not. Smart ones still wouldn't apply, since most who signed on landed in jail or the hospital or the morgue. Word got around.

As for Eric and Joseph, they were worn out. Exhaustion mixed with exhilaration as they waited to catch a red-eye flight to Little Rock. When they boarded a half-empty plane, sleep was impossible. They were still too excited after realizing the investigation was over at last. Munching peanuts, Eric thanked Joseph for saving his life again, "How many times has it been?"

"My friend," said Joseph, "You keep getting into so much trouble! You always need me to bail you out." They both laughed. Eric spilled peanuts all over the cabin.

"I've got to phone Sarah!" Eric fumbled for his cell phone. "Guess it's alright on a police jet!"

She was groggy from lack of sleep when she answered. "Eric, is that you?"

"Yes, Sarah! The case is closed! And I'm fine. And I mean it. I am fine."

He heard her shout a praise to God. Then Sarah said, "Will you be back in time for our next appointment with the counselor?"

Eric smiled and said, "I wouldn't miss it for the world! Now, please get some rest. We are at last out of the woods! Your prayers were so important."

He clicked off and settled back into the plane seat. He turned to Joseph and said, "Joseph?"

"Yes?"

"When did you realize Sonya was the one for you?"

"Ah, that was a special time for me. Once I was talking with her and she looked at me with those beautiful dark eyes and said, 'Joseph, when are we going to get married?' That was when I knew!" Eric and Joseph both laughed and spilled more peanuts.

The flight attendant came to a crunching stop, "Looks like you two have had enough nuts for this flight." She continued walking with a hint of disgust. Joseph and Eric looked at one another. Eric spoke up sheepishly, "We're really sorry, ma'am."

They settled into their seats but couldn't sleep. The excitement of the day was too much, so they rehearsed the events of the chase in detail. Although the case now resided with the authorities, they would be called on to testify in court.

"Joseph? Do you know what excited me most about this case?"

"What?"

"How well the plan worked. It was dangerous, but you had my back and that meant everything to me."

Joseph just smiled and shrugged his shoulders. He said nothing.

Landing at the Little Rock airport, Eric called the garage where his pickup was being repaired.

"Yep. Yir vehicle is ready, Mr. Bonfield. Want me to deliver it?"

"That would be great. Can you come to the airport?"

"No problem."

Joseph was anxious to get home, so he caught a taxi.

The mechanic pulled up and handed Eric his keys. "Mr. Bonfield, you sure do live an exciting life! I'm proud to work on your truck."

"Well, I'm glad to have such an excellent mechanic to keep my truck going!"

With truck wheels under him, Eric felt he was driving a dream. *I don't like sedans!* Eric headed straight to Sarah's farm. He had one thing on his mind. He promised Sarah to be there for her in one piece, to hold her in his arms, and kiss her . . . no problem!

Chapter 23

Although thoroughly tired, Eric drove without stopping. *Got to get to Sarah's farm.* Sarah threw open the door when she heard the familiar tires on her driveway. She came running as he got out of his trusty steed. Sarah leaped into his arms and hugged him as if she would never let him go. Then, suddenly, she released him and stepped back. She stood silent for a moment, then she burst into tears, and sobbed, "Oh, Eric! I love you so much!"

Eric's heart skipped a couple beats. He scooped her into his arms and held her aloft just as he had done before he left on his dangerous journey. Words finally came to him and he said, "Sarah, I love you with all my heart!"

They sat at her kitchen table staring into each other's eyes as he related the amazing events that led to the capture of the Overshoot gang.

Sarah asked, "Why did the Overshoot bunch do so much killing? It seems so weird to put that much energy into preserving a small mine?"

Eric thought about this for a moment before answering. "These people are first and foremost criminals. They're ignorant of geology but thought they could expand their illegal business of disposing of toxic chemicals to include mining. Discovering an old geology report about the area stirred their greed. By hiring a cunning lawyer, they devised a shrewd plan to get control of the mineral rights. Their ignorance of geological facts cost the lives of other people. This isn't the first case of its kind. When gangsters barge into a technical industry, lots of people can get hurt."

Closing the tale, Eric's eyelids began to droop. Sarah forced him to swallow another cup of coffee and sent him to his pickup. "I don't want you to have an accident; not after all the danger you've come through. So, you go straight to your apartment and sleep!" Sarah demanded. "You have to meet your boss. Sean McDonnell will be so excited to hear your story."

"Sean McDonnell excited? I never thought it'd happen!"

"He called me when he heard the criminals were caught. He could hardly talk; he was so exhilarated."

"Do tell." Eric made an attempt to smile. He feebly kissed Sarah and groggily made it to his pickup. He nearly spilled coffee as he opened the door.

Sarah marched over and shoved a stick of gum in his mouth. "Now chew that and swig coffee all the way home."

He obediently nodded and started the engine. "I can make it. I must. This whole affair is almost over."

She watched as his pickup maneuvered out of her driveway and headed the correct direction toward town. She shook her head and yawned. Now she could sleep. Stan would understand if she came in late to work.

Eric made it to his apartment and collapsed onto his bed.

In all too short a time, the alarm went off. After a shower to help him wake up, Eric grabbed a very late breakfast and paid his morning visit to the nurse next door. "I know you think I'm about healed up, but the last few days have put some strain on my body. Could you do the honors one more time?"

Alice laughed and bandaged him for a final time. "I hope you're done with this dangerous stuff for a while."

"You and me both!"

After he dressed for the field, Eric set off to report the good news to Sean McDonnell. When Eric arrived at McDonnell's office, the businessman had been working for three hours. *What a serious guy and on a Saturday too.*

They sat around a table as Eric reported details of the chase. Eric watched a huge grin stretch across Sean's face.

"Eric, you've done a fantastic job. My attorneys tell me that the contract and will have been voided. There'll be a giant bonus for all the extra work and dangers you've faced."

"Thanks. But I've a question. Would you like to check out the mine site to verify that there really is an ore body like the Overshoot people believed?"

"You bet! Let's go now!"

They drove in Sean's pickup. The vehicle was decades older than Eric's and rode like a hay wagon. The chassis transferred every road bump to its passengers. Eric couldn't help but wonder why McDonnell drove such a beast. After traveling a short distance, Sean answered the unspoken question.

"Eric, just in case you wonder, I never spend money on unnecessary frills. This old crate takes me back and forth to work. My wife, Joyce, has a nice car which she uses all the time, and we take it on trips. It's all a matter of priorities."

"I understand. And I agree that some things are a lot more important than others." He didn't elaborate.

McDonnell was especially chatty as they drove to his farm. "This whole mess with the illegal mining company had me on edge. I'm glad to be free of those people. And I feel so much relief that you weren't badly hurt."

Eric nodded, but his eyes fought to stay open as the antique pickup jostled him from side to side.

When they arrived at the mine site, it was abandoned. Equipment stood idle. The wind made a low whistling noise over the inactive pit. They walked around the bulldozed area as they tried to find any trace of valuable minerals.

As they walked, Sean talked. "You know, when I heard of the false will and was told I inherited the farm, the first thing I did was contact a livestock auction and arrange to sell the small herd of cattle that Abe kept. I didn't want them to suffer from lack of care, since no one lived on the farm. Other than that, I didn't change anything on the property. The auction called me this week and said they held onto the herd in case something came up. I told them that I had no legal rights now and that some of the McDonnell family might want those critters back. After all, the will gives the property to them."

"Good plan," said Eric. He was busily scanning the site for tell-tale evidence of vanadinite. The bright red color should stick out like a flare, at least to a geologist. They tramped around for a half hour. The sun glared at them and sweat ran down their backs and faces.

Finally, Eric spotted a few flashes of red in rocks outside the dump site. Sure enough, vanadinite crystals sparkled in the sunlight, but they were in very thin veins. Eric traced them until they thinned to nothing. Nothing about the veins seemed to lead to any larger ore body on Abe's property.

After looking over the entire area, Eric said, in his most analytical tone, "Mr. McDonnell, it's my professional opinion these guys duped themselves. Somebody found this old publication and located where the specimens came from. But they didn't read the full report. They weren't geologists and missed the important parts. I guess they caught mineral fever.

"When I first studied the report's map, I didn't read far enough to see what the geologist thought about his discoveries. Since then, I've read the whole report from cover to cover. The author clearly states in one spot that he found vanadinite. I think the Overshoot gang saw this but didn't read any further. If they'd read the full report, they might have seen that the minerals occur only in thin veins. The veins don't lead to any significant ore body. Yes, vanadinite is mined in Magnet Cove, but the veins on Abe's property seem to be only small offshoots from the main source, which isn't on your land.

"It looks as if the Overshoot gang barked up the wrong tree. It's awful that so many people died or were injured because of their oversight or lack of geological knowledge combined with greed. These people expected a spectacular red 'gold mine' that turned out to be nothing more than a dump!"

"You know, Eric, I'm glad to know this. You've proved this mine is my mine and not theirs. Funny thing is, the original will didn't give it directly to me anyway. Besides, I don't really want it!"

They both laughed.

"I saw the original will. Abe's will didn't specifically have my name on it! The will's language is vague enough so his closest relatives, the nieces and nephews, will likely be the real recipients. I don't need or want this property. I've got too much to keep me busy as it is. In fact, I think the largest share will go to Josephine. I've heard she'll pull through with few complications."

"That's great news. She deserves some good breaks."

Eric smiled and shook Sean's hand, "You're a good person, Mr. McDonnell. I respect you and your integrity. Honest people are not easy to find."

"Well, let me say that brave, private detective-geologists aren't easy to find either!" And they both laughed.

"You know, there's something I still don't understand. Why did the Overshoot crooks draft a fake will to make you the beneficiary of the farm, minus the mineral rights? I know they thought there'd be money to be made in vanadinite. But why you as beneficiary of the farm?"

Sean considered this for a moment before answering. "My guess is the Overshoot gang thought I wouldn't be concerned for this little patch of land and might pay no attention to their mine. They probably thought Abe's other relatives would put up a bigger stink about having a mine on their property if the original will was in force."

"Sounds reasonable, but they misjudged you, didn't they?"

"You bet! I don't tolerate shady deals."

Reflecting, Eric said, "You know, this whole scheme of creating illegal dump sites might have gone on indefinitely except for two things."

"What's that?"

"They became greedy when they discovered a valuable mineral deposit might exist where they wanted to start a new dump. Not being geologists, they read only part of the geologist's report. They probably looked online and saw how valuable vanadium is and greed took over. Their second mistake was messing with you!"

They laughed again.

Eric continued, "Cleanup of this site will be a huge job. The Arkansas EPA and federal government will assess the damage and see what needs to be done. Fortunately, Overshoot only used a small part of the area to dig a hole and bury the contaminants. Your farm may become famous, but not for good reasons."

"I understand. I'm not certain what my relatives will do with the property. They can decide that among themselves. Maybe they'll bring Abe's cattle back and have someone manage the farmland."

Eric stood still for a moment and stared at the rock face laced with gleaming red vanadinite veins. He smiled and turned to Sean, "I have an idea. Take a look at that shear rock face. I'm not a specialist in decorative stone, but I'll bet some beautiful building material could come out of this mine. The striking red veins cutting across the face of the light tan limestone might be a real discovery for the Arkansas decorative stone industry. The McDonnell family might have a "gold mine" of sorts after all!"

"You know, I think you may have something there! I could see this as facing for a new bank I'm building in Hot Springs. I'll suggest this to my relatives and ask a friend of mine in the construction business what she thinks. Eric, you may have found a use for an otherwise useless hole in the ground!?

"That bit of geological consulting is free. Just don't ask me to do more than that. I'm not a quarry guy!"

They both laughed. Sean said, "Actually, I'm going to round up your fee a bit. And how about putting you on retainer? I never know when your skills may build my business."

"Let's just say that I'm available on a piece work consulting basis. I never like to be tied down. That's an independence I got from my dad."

"I've got your phone number, you know!"

Changing the subject, Eric said, "I'm told that, in addition to the Overshoot gang, the killers hired by Overshoot will all live to face serious charges for their murderous acts. A number will be tried in other states as well. It seems a real rat's nest of criminals got caught when they took jobs with Overshoot Mining. This has been a grueling experience for us both. I hope you can relax after all this."

"Me too! Would you like to have a very late lunch?"

Eric remembered that Sean's lunches tended to be on the light side, and it was nearly time for the next counseling session. "Maybe some other time, Mr. McDonnell. Right now, I've got a date with two women!" The two men shook hands again.

Back in the office, Joseph was catching up on some projects left hanging while he and Eric closed in on the Overshoot criminals. Although it was Saturday and her day off, Megan stopped by to hear Joseph spin the tale of how the bad guys were captured.

After listening to Joseph's lengthy discourse, Megan said, "You know Eric and Sarah are having another premarital counseling session this afternoon, don't you?"

"I've heard that things are getting serious." He smiled. "You know, I'm ready for some quiet consulting work."

Megan agreed. "Right! These extra Saturday work binges are tiring. I've got a ton of e-mails to catch up on. Get ready for some of that 'quiet consulting work'!"

Joseph rolled his eyes and sighed.

Then the phone rang. Megan picked it up, listened, and frowned at Joseph. She shook her head, covered the receiver, and said, "Now I've heard everything!"

About the Author

Max W. Reams, Ph.D., taught geology at Olivet Nazarene University, Bourbonnais, IL, for five decades. He is a Certified Life Coach, speaker, Trainer for Life Innovations, Inc., and author of *Geology of Illinois State Parks, Oil on my Hands, Before your Journey, and On the Journey.*